MW00965996

Night Mare

Night Mare

by
Vicki Kamida

Random House 🏠 New York

http://www.randomhouse.com/

Library of Congress Cataloging-in-Publication Data
Kamida, Vicki.   Night mare / by Vicki Kamida.
p. cm. — (Random House riders)   SUMMARY: Thirteen-year-old
Janet's dream becomes a nightmare when she discovers that the
magnificent white horse visiting her at night is a darkly magical
beast that can never be tamed.
ISBN 0-679-88628-1 (trade)
ISBN 0-679-98628-6 (lib. bdg.)
[1. Horses—Fiction. 2. Horsemanship—Fiction. 3. Ghosts—Fiction.]
I. Title. II. Series. PZ7.K126746Ni 1997b [Fic]—dc21   97–2120

Printed in the United States of America
10 9 8 7 6 5 4 3 2 1

For Cliff

Night Mare

CHAPTER ONE

Ten minutes into riding class, Janet's mount, Sugar, rose up on his back hooves and dumped her to the ground. It was the third time that morning, and as she picked herself up from the dirt, Janet was anything but happy.

"That does it, Sugar," she said under her breath. "You want to fight? We'll fight."

She remounted and jabbed her heels—hard—into Sugar's belly. The horse took off somewhere between a hard trot and a canter, barreling past the other girls who were also taking their lessons in the ring.

"Janet Marshall! Control your mount! You'll never get points with that form!"

Janet cringed. The voice came from the bleachers. It was Connie Caston, the stable's trainer. Leave it to Connie to catch her in the act of kicking Sugar. Nothing got past her eagle eyes.

"Get over here, Janet," Connie said, her voice sharp. "I want to talk to you."

While the other girls went on with their lesson, Janet steered Sugar toward the bleachers.

"What is going on with you?" Connie asked. "From the way you're riding, it looks like you've forgotten the first rule of horsemanship."

"Never ride angry," Janet replied.

"Exactly," Connie said sharply. "So take a deep breath and count to three and then tell me what the problem is."

Janet didn't know where to start. She and Connie both knew that riding Sugar, a school horse, was about as much fun as riding a mule. The horse was stubborn and old and tired. His form may have worked for kids who didn't know much about riding, but in just three months Janet was facing her first competition. And the last thing she wanted was to go through it on a lame horse like Sugar. Unfortunately, since she didn't have a horse of her own, she didn't have much choice.

"It's just that Hallie and Becky get to ride their own horses, and I'm stuck with Sugar," Janet explained. "There's no way I'll win a ribbon in the season opener."

A week ago, Connie had gathered all the girls in Janet's age group and level—from novice to maiden— and told them about the season opener, a special two-day event to be held in February at the Equestrian Center in Burbank. San Pascual Stables, where Janet rode, was cosponsoring a class. Janet's best friend, Hallie, was going to ride, and so were Becky and Cody and Aloe, three other girls from the stables. The problem was, they all had their own horses. Connie had let Janet train on Sugar as a favor. But it wasn't turning out to be much of one.

"With an attitude like that," Connie said, "you're right. You won't. Now get back there and keep going with your lesson."

Her friend Hallie shot her an encouraging look as she rejoined the other girls. "Ready for another dumping?" Hallie asked, her red curls bouncing from side to side as she posted. "I think Sugar's still got some life left in him. Maybe he'll put you on the ground one more time."

"Very funny," Janet said.

Hallie could afford to joke. She had Duke to ride. Ahead of them in the ring, Becky maneuvered her prize stallion, MacDougal, through a set of lead changes. Hallie went off to follow the commands Connie was giving from the side and did a great job. But when Janet tried the same simple moves—trot on the right lead, now trot left—Sugar got tripped up. Janet lost her balance and nearly fell from the saddle again.

"Thanks a lot," she muttered. "Thanks a whole lot!"

By the end of the lesson, Janet was ready to give up. The season opener would be her first horse show ever. But there was no way she'd do anything but bomb on Sugar.

On the way back to Sugar's stall, Janet passed

Yankee, a chestnut beauty. Yankee was nearly sixteen hands high and had the most amazing form. Ever since she'd started training Sugar, Janet had caught herself looking longingly in Yankee's direction. Now, *there* was a horse with spirit!

Yankee had grown up barrel racing, which gave him a feisty spirit and good legs but no instincts for jumps or moves on the flat. For a year now, his owner had been training him in equitation, or "eq," as it was called. And it was definitely paying off. Yankee had gone from being green to being a solid ride.

If only she could ride a horse like Yankee in the season opener, then she would win a ribbon for sure. But that just wasn't possible. Yankee's owner didn't let him do school rides. And there was no way Janet could afford to buy a horse. She wasn't like Hallie or Becky, whose parents had bought horses for them. Her mom and dad reminded her that they were taking every possible opportunity to save for her college education. Owning a horse was simply out of the question. Period. End of discussion.

But that didn't stop her from dreaming. She wanted a horse so badly! While she groomed Sugar, Janet imagined mounting Yankee and putting him through his moves. Feeling him take the paces, knowing he'd handle the jumps and cues. It would be incredible! Just to ride a real horse, one that didn't stumble and refuse jumps. One that was predictable!

She was halfway through grooming Sugar when she

realized that Connie had stopped by Yankee's stall and was talking to Mrs. Wrubel, the horse's owner.

"I just wish I could find someone who wanted to buy half my partnership," Mrs. Wrubel was saying. "I can't afford to keep him all by myself. But, unfortunately, there aren't many people who see Yankee's potential."

"I'll ask around," Connie told her. "The price is completely reasonable. Most people recognize a good deal when they see one."

"I hope so," Mrs. Wrubel said. "Otherwise, I'll have to sell Yankee, and I really don't want to do that. Not after all the time I've spent training him. He'll be a great competitor. He just needs someone who cares."

Janet felt her ears perk up, just the way a horse's might if he smelled a carrot nearby. It wasn't often that a partnership in a horse came up for sale. And an affordable one was even harder to find. She might have a chance to own Yankee after all! She finished feeding Sugar, shut him in his stall, and went next door.

"Excuse me," she said. "But I heard you talking to Connie just now. Is it true you're selling half your partnership?"

"It's either that or let go of the horse completely," Mrs. Wrubel said. "Why do you ask?"

"I might want to buy it," Janet said. "I mean, if I can afford it, that is."

Mrs. Wrubel smiled. "What's your name?"

"Janet. Janet Marshall. I ride a school horse here. But—you know...."

"He's old and stubborn and tired," Mrs. Wrubel guessed. "And I bet his name is Sugar."

"Exactly," Janet said. "How much were you asking for the partnership?"

"Fifteen hundred," she said. "Plus half the expenses, of course."

Fifteen hundred! It wasn't a lot for a half ownership, but it was a lot more than she could afford. Unless…

"I know this may sound strange, but could I possibly pay you in installments?" she asked.

It was a crazy idea, since any horse owner would want the money up front. What if something happened to the horse? How could she count on Janet to keep paying? And what if she wanted to move away? What happened then? But she kept silent, unable to bear the thought of letting Yankee slip through her fingers.

Janet thought of her savings account. So she'd wipe it out. Wasn't it worth it? One look at Yankee told her it was. "I have some money for a down payment. About five hundred. After that, I could give you a little every month, on top of expenses."

Mrs. Wrubel actually thought about the idea. "Kind of like layaway?" she asked.

Janet nodded.

"It's something to consider, I suppose." She paused. "I don't want to sell to just anyone. Yankee needs an owner who understands what a great horse he can be."

"Oh, I do!" Janet said. She reached out to pet the horse, amazed that maybe he could be hers. Yankee gazed down at Janet with warm brown eyes and nick-ered softly. "I've been watching him, and I can tell he's smart."

"That he is," Mrs. Wrubel agreed. "Plus, he seems to like you. Okay, Janet. Let's see if we can work it out. Why don't you ask your parents, and I'll think about it. Don't forget that you'll have to come up with money for stabling and the vet and all that other stuff. It gets expensive."

Janet didn't care. She knew that somehow she'd find a way to work it out.

"Oh, thank you," she said, practically hugging Mrs. Wrubel. "Thank you so much! You won't be sorry!"

While Mrs. Wrubel finished grooming Yankee, Janet rushed off to tell Hallie. "I'm going to have my own horse!" she shouted when she got to Duke's stall. "Can you believe it? My very own horse!"

Hallie looked up from picking at Duke's shoes. "You're kidding, right?" she said, snapping her gum loudly. "What, did Connie give you Sugar out of total sympathy?"

"Yeah, right." Janet swung from a rafter in Duke's stall. "Nope, it's even better. Mrs. Wrubel's selling half her partnership in Yankee. And guess who's gonna buy it?"

"No way!" Hallie shrieked. "Marshall, that's amazing! But how are you going to afford it? I mean, even a cheap partnership means you have to cover board and all that other stuff."

"I know." The reality of how expensive it could be was slowly starting to sink in. "I'm going to ask my parents," Janet said. "They'll help."

Secretly, Janet wasn't so sure. But she didn't even want to think about their saying no. They had to see how important it was for her to own a horse. And a chance like this didn't come along very often. They just had to say yes.

"Wow, Marshall. If you ride Yankee, you might even beat me in eq."

"Watch out, Hallie," Janet warned. "'Cause I just might!"

Janet waited for Hallie to finish up with Duke. Then the two girls walked home together along Arroyo Boulevard. Below them, the Arroyo Seco, a long, wide canyon with a stream running through it, cut through the valley. High canyons rose on the other side of the stream.

When she had first moved to Pasadena from San Francisco, Janet was in awe of the arroyo. She'd never seen anything like it. Groves of sycamores grew along the banks of the stream, along with birch trees, live oaks, wild sage, and creosote bushes.

In some ways, the arroyo scared her: it felt so empty and so vacant. She could hear the birds moving among the fallen leaves. Up above, large hawks circled the sky, then perched on the canyon's cliffs. Her house looked like a toy amid the deep, thick brambles of the arroyo.

"So how are you gonna tell your parents?" Hallie asked, blowing a large bubble that popped and plastered her face. "Is it the direct approach, or something more subtle, like making them breakfast and then begging on your hands and knees?"

"Like that would work," Janet said. They both knew her parents could see her coming a mile away. "Nope. I think I'm just going to have to come out and tell them: Mom, Dad, you've got to let me do this. Or else."

"Or else what?"

"Or else I'll be mad at you for the rest of my life," she said.

"Yeah, right. Parents *expect* you to be mad at them for the rest of their lives. That's why they're parents. See ya, Marshall, and good luck."

Hallie peeled off toward her street, leaving Janet to head the rest of the way home by herself. How could they say no? she thought. They had to see how important this was to her. Yankee was an incredible horse. Fifteen hundred was nothing compared to how much he would be worth once he started winning. If her mother and father knew anything about horses, they'd know what a great investment it was.

Unfortunately for Janet, she was the only one besides her grandfather with real horse blood, as her grandfather called it. Even though her father had grown up on a ranch, he had never gone back after leaving for college.

At least Hallie knew what it felt like to love horses. And Connie had given her a really lucky break by hiring her to do grooming and mucking. That meant she could actually take lessons. Even if they were on Sugar.

But now she had the chance to do one better. Now she could actually own a horse of her very own. It meant more to her than anything else in the world. Her parents would just have to see that.

When she got home, she found her parents at the back of the house, having a cup of coffee in the large, modern kitchen. "How was school, Scooter?" Janet's father asked, putting the lid back on a pot on the stove. "Make any brilliant discoveries?"

She went straight to the refrigerator and took a long sip of juice straight from the carton. If she was going to discuss Yankee with her parents, she needed fortification. "Not exactly," she said. "Just the usual. RNA, DNA, my own private theory of evolution."

"Very good, very good," her father said, clearly not listening to her answer.

While her father stood at the stove, cooking dinner, her mother pored over blueprints at the kitchen table. Both her parents had intense careers—her dad was a journalist and her mom was an architect—which was good because that meant they didn't interfere too much in her life. But sometimes Janet wished her dad would ask her something—anything—besides his usual question about brilliant discoveries. And that her mother would take a time-out from her blueprints.

Janet sat down across from her mom and waited for her to look up.

"What is it, honey?" Mrs. Marshall asked, preoccupied with checking a measurement. "Something wrong?"

"Mom, how can you tell if something's wrong when you're not even looking at me?"

Liz Marshall glanced up and smiled at her daughter. "Because I've known you for thirteen years and I have expert radar for detecting that cloud that sometimes appears over your head. Right now it's big and dark and threatening to burst wide open into a storm. What's up?"

"Dad?" Janet glanced over at her father.

"Honey?"

"Can you sit down please?"

"This sounds serious. Let me just drain the pasta before it overcooks."

When both her parents were sitting with her at the table, she took a deep breath.

"I know you've told me I can't have my own horse, and I know you said we can't afford to board one, but I have a once-in-a-lifetime chance to buy a partnership in a horse at the stables. It's really affordable, and the owner says I can pay her a little every month and still ride the horse. I guess I was hoping that since this isn't really buying a horse, at least not a whole horse, just a partnership in a horse, you might think about it. I mean, it's the most affordable way for me to have my own ride, you know.

"And, Mom, if you saw Yankee, you'd know this was worth it. He's so incredible! He's not really young, but he's a solid ride, and he's got a lot of good years left in him. I just know that with a little bit of training I can get him to win championships. And besides, the stable is sponsoring a class in the season opener in February, and all the riders from there can enter for practically nothing, and I bet, I just bet that on Yankee I can win at least three blues—"

"Janet, whoa. Slow down there a minute. Who's Yankee, and what's a partnership, and what's it actually going to cost?" her father asked. "I want the numbers, kiddo."

"You're not going to like this," she said, realizing that she'd done the calculations in her head, but never out loud.

"For some reason, I already knew that," her father said. "So give us the dirt."

"Okay. The partnership is fifteen hundred, total," she said. "Mrs. Wrubel's willing to let me pay that off little by little. I have enough saved up to make a pretty big contribution—probably five hundred dollars or so."

"Janet!" Her mother dropped the pen she'd been holding. "How have you managed to save that much money?"

"I put a little bit away every month from my allowance," she explained. "And I save my Christmas and birthday money from Grandma and Grandpa. And then there's my lunch money." Her parents didn't know it, but for the past two years, she'd been saving a dollar a day out of the money her mother gave her for lunch. So what if she had to drink water instead of soda? It was worth it. "I saved two hundred dollars right there."

"Janet!" Now her mother was exasperated.

"I know, I know." Somehow, she just had to find a way to explain to her parents just how important this was. "Mom, horses are my life," she said. "You know that."

"I'm beginning to realize just how true that is."

"Okay, let's get back to the numbers," her father said, obviously trying to calm them all down. "Say you actually could cover the partnership, which I'm not so sure about, since you'll still be left owing Mrs. Wrubel almost a thousand dollars, and who knows how long she'll wait to be paid. What about feed and stabling and all that?"

This was going to be the hard part. There was no way to get around it: sharing in stabling the horse would cost her two hundred a month. Then there was the training and the shoes. She'd have to share half the expense of all those bills, including the vet.

"Well…" Janet began.

"Well what?" her mother asked.

"Well, I was hoping that you could help me out with it."

"How much?" her father said.

She braced herself for their reaction. "Three hundred a month," she said finally.

"Three hundred!" her mother exclaimed.

"That's a lot of money," her father added.

"I know." Of course her dad was right. Three hundred dollars was a fortune. "But I can help. We'll cancel my allowance. I'll do extra chores."

"And there's always the recycling." It was a joke, but her father wasn't smiling. "That would bring in a lot extra. Janet, you're not seeing this realistically. No matter how much you think you can contribute, that's a heavy responsibility you're asking your mother and me to take on. We can't promise to pay to stable Yankee unless we're sure we can afford it. Right now, all our extra money is going to your college fund. It's all we can do to keep up with that, and both of us really want you to have that opportunity. I'm sorry, sweetie, but I'm afraid we can't afford it."

Can't afford it.

Just the words she'd been afraid to hear. Janet knew they weren't poor, and she certainly wasn't deprived, but when she thought about the other girls at the stables— the ones like Becky whose parents gave them everything they wanted—how could she help but feel sorry for herself?

"Mom, Dad, are you sure? Please think about it, at least overnight. I know it's a lot of money, but there must be some way. Maybe you could save less for college? I just can't let a chance like this go by. You've got to understand."

"I'm sorry, Janet, but no means no." Her mother's voice was soft but firm.

"But Mom—"

"Don't 'but Mom' me." Her mother got up from the table and put her blueprints away. "End of discussion."

Janet could see that her mother wasn't going to budge, so she appealed to her father. "Dad?"

"Janet, I'm sorry, but we just can't afford it. Which would you rather have—the chance to go to a good college, or being able to ride your own horse?"

To Janet, the answer was obvious. Of course she'd vote for the horse. Who in her right mind wouldn't?

CHAPTER TWO

"*No means no*," she heard her mother saying over and over again. And her father's words were equally hard to forget. "*I'm sorry, Janet, but we just can't afford it.*"

It was late, and her parents were already in bed, but Janet couldn't sleep. Instead, she kept thinking about Yankee. And how he'd never be hers.

Never.

She threw off the covers. Toby, the stuffed toy horse her grandparents had given her when she was five, fell to the ground. Janet picked him up and played with his fur, the way she used to as a child when something really upsetting had happened.

What was she going to do? She couldn't bear the idea of facing Mrs. Wrubel. She tossed and turned for what felt like hours. Finally, she decided that she would leave a message on Mrs. Wrubel's answering machine the next day. And hopefully, Mrs. Wrubel wouldn't be home. She knew it was lame, but she would die if she had to tell Mrs. Wrubel to her face.

Janet moaned and pulled the quilt over her again.

Sometime around two in the morning, she heard a noise at the window beside her bed. She looked up and saw the most incredible sight: there, with its face pressed to the window, was a beautiful creature, all white, with a flowing mane and intense black eyes. It was the most gorgeous horse Janet had ever seen.

"What on earth—"

The horse nudged its nose under her open window, then neighed softly, its breath steaming up the window glass, its head beckoning to her.

"You want me to come play?" Janet guessed.

The horse nodded.

Janet went to the window and pushed it open all the way so she could reach out to pet the horse's nose. The animal lowered its head to receive Janet's touch. Then it backed away. Janet leaned out the window, but the horse had stepped too far off for her to touch it.

"Okay," she said aloud. "I guess I'll have to come after you."

Janet opened the window wider and found herself greeted by a blast of cold air as she climbed out. The ground was freezing under her feet, but the horse was so mesmerizing that she hardly noticed. She didn't recognize the animal from the stables. Even so, it seemed healthy and cared for, with a shiny white coat and brushed mane and tail. While she circled the mare, examining it, the horse kept nudging Janet playfully with her nose and nickering to her softly in the night.

Standing there, looking at the proud, tall mare, Janet was overcome with the desire to ride her. The question was, would the horse let her?

"Here, girl," Janet said, clucking to the horse.

The horse approached as if she were interested in finding out what Janet had in mind. Janet reached out to pat her side, then spoke to her in a soft voice. "What's your name, girl? What do they call you?"

With her pale, dappled coat and her long flowing mane, the mare reminded Janet of some elegant Arabian horse, one that would have an exotic name. Then again, her white coat and blazing black eyes also called to mind cold, northern climates, blanketed with snow.

"I know," Janet said. "I'll call you Storm. So how are we going to mount you, Storm? Are you going to put up a fuss?"

She'd ridden bareback before at her grandparents' ranch, so she knew how to mount without a saddle. But whether the mare had ever been ridden bareback was another matter. Being sure not to make any sudden moves, she led Storm over to a tree stump at the back of the yard. Janet reached out for the horse's back, grabbed on to her mane, and mounted her.

She landed with a hard belly-flop on Storm's back. At first, the mare was startled and stepped forward, but Janet quickly swung her leg around, grabbed on to the mare's neck, and firmly straddled the horse. She was on!

"There you go," she said, patting the mare's side to calm her down. "You're a good girl, aren't you?"

The horse craned her neck around to look at Janet with her startling black eyes. Then she raised her head, cocked back her ears, and neighed—loudly now—into the dark.

By now, Janet was almost as excited as Storm. It wasn't enough to be sitting on Storm's back. She wanted to see what it felt like to ride her. Janet nudged the horse's side lightly with her heels to see if she would accept the cue. Storm took an easy step forward. Using her hands on the mare's mane to guide her, Janet made simple circles around the backyard. Then she coaxed Storm into a trot. The mare took the gait effortlessly, hardly bouncing Janet at all.

"It's like we were meant to be together," she whispered as they continued circling the yard. "Oh, Storm, I wish you were mine."

She didn't want the ride to end. As she went around and around, she started to imagine the competitions she could enter. Maybe someday she could even hire a sire to have Storm's colts.

A moment later, Janet reminded herself to cut it out. A horse like this had to have an owner. She wasn't a stray dog or something that Janet could just take in. Instead of dreaming about competing on Storm, she should try to find out whom she belonged to.

Janet pulled Storm to a halt. She was about to swing

her leg over and hop off when the horse started to squirm. "Oh, come on, horse. Let me off."

But the mare had other ideas. Every time the horse stood still, Janet got ready to leap off. And every time she was close to dismounting, the horse moved, forcing her to hold on—or risk falling to the ground. She was just about ready to throw herself off and risk a seriously sore ankle when suddenly Storm had another idea. Before Janet could stop her, she was bolting toward the street, with Janet holding fast on to her back.

"Whoa!" Janet cried. "Slow down!"

She pulled back on Storm's mane, but it was no use. Before, the mare had been willing to follow commands. Now it was as if she was possessed. Storm picked up speed, going from a trot to a gallop. Janet dug in her heels and pulled on her mane, but nothing she could do would stop her. Instead, they were racing down the street, past darkened houses where the lawns were still wet from the nighttime sprinklers.

Janet wove her fingers into the long white hairs of Storm's mane and held on for dear life. Racing down the street, with the wind blowing through her mane, Storm really lived up to her name. Janet clung to her back, but for some reason, she wasn't afraid. If she started to slip, the mare slowed enough for her to regain her balance. Every one of their movements worked together, so that even when Storm raced down a steep path into the darkened arroyo, Janet held her breath but didn't panic. With sure footing, the mare clambered down the rocky trail and headed straight for the creek. It was as if she had a goal in mind—and nothing, not even Janet, could stop her from reaching it.

All around her, Janet could hear the arroyo's mysterious, nighttime sounds. Owls whooped from the branches of the oaks, high above. Small animals rustled in the dense underbrush below. In the trees on either side, shapes moved, jumped from branch to branch, and called out in chirps and chitters to one another. Janet held her breath, but the mare had no fear. Instead, she crossed the creek with a sure foot and scaled the banks of the river on the other side.

Storm made her way through the fields either by some sixth sense or magic or both. There didn't seem to be a trail, but even so, Storm seemed to know exactly where they were going. When they entered a thick grove of sycamores, the horse slowed down a bit. On either side of her, Janet heard the same mysterious and frightening noises. What was in the dark? Would something jump out at them? Storm certainly didn't seem to be afraid. The horse kept her head down, her ears set back, and her nose pitched forward.

They headed deeper into the arroyo. Around her, Janet felt the air come alive, the way it did right before a storm. The hair on her arms stood up, only it wasn't from the cold. In the distance, she heard the sound of rushing water, and as Storm brought them closer to it, Janet saw an amazing waterfall, cascading down from a break in the canyon wall. In the heights above the waterfall, Janet spotted darkened caves cut into the rock. She heard wings beating and looked up to see a flock of bats flying from cave to cave.

Soon the path veered from the canyon wall and opened out onto another wide trail. Again Storm picked up speed, and Janet had to reposition herself firmly on the mare's back and bury her hands in her mane so that she wouldn't lose her balance. The wind rushed through her hair. The trees went by in a darkened blur. Janet lost all sense of time and place, thinking only of this wild adventure in this wild place, wondering when it would end but hoping it never would.

Suddenly, she spotted trouble ahead. A huge old oak had fallen across the trail, its trunk rising nearly four feet above the ground. Janet held her breath. Without reins, she had no way to guide Storm over the jump. Could the horse make it?

Janet closed her eyes and prepared for the worst. The trunk loomed closer—and closer. Soon, there was no more time. Storm had to leap. Or else.

Suddenly, Janet felt the mare's front legs leave the ground. A moment later, they were airborne in the most effortless jump Janet had ever seen. She soared over the trunk on the mare's back and landed, hardly jarring her at all, on the other side.

"Wow," she whispered.

She'd never seen a horse with Storm's abilities. Her stride was even and effortless, her jumping skills incredible. If only the mare were hers, there was no telling where they might go together.

Storm led Janet farther down the trail, slowing her pace to an even trot. Suddenly, Storm stopped short. They were in a wild thicket now, overhung with branches. "What's up, girl?" Janet asked her.

Storm nickered softly, then turned to her left. There, barely visible in the dark, was a narrow trail that led off the main path. Janet would never have noticed it if Storm hadn't stopped. The mare stood at the edge of the thick sagebrush, while Janet shoved aside the branches that had flown into her face.

"Where are you taking me?" she asked. "Is this some kind of wild-goose chase?"

It was as if the path were from some fairy tale and Storm was the magical horse that was meant to find it. The way in was thick and overgrown…all Janet could think about was *Sleeping Beauty*. Under her knees, Storm's muscles stiffened in determination. Somehow, some way, Storm meant to get through. Janet realized her curiosity was as strong as Storm's determination. She was going with her.

She dug her heels into Storm's side. "Come on," she said. "Let's go."

But Storm had other ideas. She turned, gave Janet one last, lingering look with her large black eyes, then raised her front legs high in the air and dumped Janet on the ground in a heap.

CHAPTER THREE

*J*anet awoke with a start. Her mother was shaking her awake. It was morning and the sun was streaming through her bedroom window.

Her open bedroom window.

"Janet, what's gotten into you?" her mother asked. "You're never this hard to wake up! Come on. Your father's leaving for work in twenty minutes. If you're not ready by then, you'll have to wait for the bus." Before she left, she leaned over to kiss Janet good morning and give her an extra hug. "You know your father and I wish we could help out with Yankee, don't you?"

Janet nodded sleepily. "Uh-huh," she said. She knew her mother was trying to make up with her, but all she could think about was the white mare and their midnight ride. The last thing she remembered was being dumped on the path. Had it all been a dream, then? Could it be that she'd never taken that ride?

"And you're okay with this?"

"Sure," Janet murmured. She sat up and stared at the open window. "Listen, Mom, did you open the window this morning for some reason?"

Her mother looked confused. "No. Why?"

"Because I'm pretty sure I closed it last night."

"Huh." Her mother shrugged and picked up her briefcase. "I'm off. I'll be back at six-thirty. There's chicken defrosting in the sink. Leonard's coming for dinner tonight, so if you do go down to the stables after school, please be home on time, and that means on time to wash up, too. Okay?"

"Okay."

Janet stumbled out of bed and went to the window. Everything in the backyard looked normal—same old clothesline, same old view of the arroyo. Only the arroyo didn't look the same to her, not now, not after last night.

The whole time she was getting ready for school, she kept remembering parts of the dream—the feeling of Storm as she rode her, the wind in her hair as they raced through the arroyo. If it was a dream, it had all seemed so real! She got a shiver when she thought about that path and how Storm had dumped her before they could explore it together. Why? Something was down there, Janet thought. There had to be. Something Storm didn't want her to know about.

"Yeah, right, Marshall," Janet said as she brushed her teeth. "Something some imaginary horse didn't want you to see. Get real!"

Even so, her mind was so wrapped up in what it all meant that she barely remembered getting into her dad's Volvo. When her father pulled up in front of school ten minutes later, he had to shake her awake.

"Okay, kiddo," he said. "This is as far as I go." Her father gave his daughter a quizzical look as he put the car in gear. "You okay, sweetie?" he asked.

"Sure," said Janet. "I'm fine. Why?"

"You look like you're in a daze."

"Kind of," Janet said.

"Still mad about Yankee?" he asked.

Instantly, Janet felt guilty. Until her father had mentioned it, she'd actually been thinking more about Storm than Yankee, which was crazy. Yankee was real! Now she felt sick to her stomach thinking about how embarrassing it would be to tell Mrs. Wrubel that she couldn't have the horse after all, not to mention seeing Becky's smug expression after Janet had bragged about how Yankee was basically hers. Then there was Hallie. Hallie!

Janet hated to have anyone feel sorry for her, and Hallie would most definitely feel sorry.

"Hey, Jan!" a voice called out.

Janet turned to see Hallie trotting toward her, her hands raised as if she were holding on to reins. "Ho!" she said to her imaginary horse as she stopped by Janet's side. "So?"

"So?"

"Jan! So what did they say?"

Janet made a face.

"That good, huh?" Hallie asked.

"They said they can't afford to pay for Yankee's board."

Hallie rubbed her freckled nose and made a huge bubble out of the gum in her mouth. "No way," she said in disbelief. "That's it? Just flat-out no? Not even a 'we'll think about it'?"

Janet shook her head. "Not even."

"But every parent says, 'We'll think about it.' That's parent talk for 'Let's-put-this-off-until-we've-decided-no.'"

"Not mine."

There were still five minutes before homeroom. More than anything, Janet wanted to tell Hallie about her dream, to explain to her how riding Storm had taken her mind off Yankee. But Janet had only met Hallie back in September when she'd started junior high, and even though they hung out together a lot, she still wasn't sure if they were best friends or just friends. And when she thought about it, telling Hallie about a dream she'd had was a little weird. She wouldn't want Hallie to go down to the stables and tell Becky and the others that she was acting strange or anything.

Then again…

"Listen," Janet said. "Can you keep a secret?"

Hallie blew another bubble, a big one this time. "You bet I can," she said. "What is it?"

"I had this really weird dream last night," Janet said softly. "This incredible horse came to my window and I rode it. Down into the arroyo and everything. We crossed the creek, and then the horse took me to this path. I wanted to go down there, but she dumped me and then I woke up. I don't know, Hallie. It's hard to explain. But the dream really felt real. When I woke up, my bedroom window was open. And I never leave it open at night, especially now that it's getting cold."

"Gosh, Jan," Hallie said. "It's just like a ghost story."

"Exactly," Janet said, relieved that Hallie seemed to be just as interested as she was. "Pretty freaky, huh?"

Even now, Janet shivered when she thought of Storm. "And the thing is, I keep wondering: What if there really is some wild, abandoned horse down in the arroyo? What if she's trapped and can't get out? Maybe that's what the dream's trying to tell me."

"Do you think?"

Janet didn't know what to think. This was the first time she'd actually said it out loud, that maybe Storm was real. It was a crazy idea. Or was it?

"I know one thing," Janet said. "That horse wanted me to ride her." Now that she'd said it out loud, Janet was sure of it. Why else did Storm let her mount her, and why else did she race off with Janet on her back?

Hallie chewed her gum for a moment, then grabbed Janet's arm. "Hey! I've got a great idea! After school, we'll head into the arroyo and look for Storm. Maybe we can find her."

"Yeah!" Janet agreed.

"Excitement!" Hallie said.

"Double excitement!"

Hallie trotted off to homeroom, while Janet headed down the hall toward her classroom. She realized there wasn't any logical reason to think Storm was real. The dream had just been a dream.

Or had it?

Hallie was waiting for Janet outside the school at three-thirty. "This is so cool, Jan," Hallie said. "Becky would be insanely jealous if she knew."

"But you're not going to tell her, right?" Janet said.

"No way." Hallie shook her head, making her curls bounce. "Tell that pest? And miss out on the chance to keep something really juicy from her?"

Before Janet had moved to Pasadena, Hallie and Becky had been friends. But when Hallie decided to hang out with Janet, Becky dumped her. From what Janet could tell, it still bothered Hallie, even though she and Hallie were getting along fine. The last thing she wanted was to get stuck in the middle.

"Whatever you do, please don't tell her, okay?" Janet asked. "I mean, think of what she would say."

Hallie laughed. "Yeah, she'd probably tell everyone what a stupid idea it was."

Janet frowned.

"Hey, Jan. It's okay. I can keep a secret. Really."

The girls stopped by Hallie's house so that she could drop off her book bag and change into hiking boots. Then it was on to Janet's, where they had a quick snack and a glass of juice.

"Ready?" Janet asked Hallie.

"You bet," Hallie said, popping another piece of gum into her mouth. "Lead the way, Marshall."

On the way down to the arroyo, Hallie was full of questions. "What if we really do find Storm?" she asked. "Does that mean you didn't dream your dream at all, but it was real? I mean, it's really hard to believe, you know?"

Janet did know. Part of her just really wanted to believe the dream. Because she was hoping—praying—it would come true. She couldn't help thinking how incredible it would be if they really did find Storm. She could just picture the scene: the two of them leading the mare out of the arroyo, bringing her to San Pascual, everyone's incredulous stares. She'd look for Storm's real owner, of course, but in the meantime, the mare would be hers—and only hers. And then maybe, after a few months, no one would come forward and claim Storm, and Janet would register her in her name. She'd have a horse of her very own! A horse she was meant to ride!

"Isn't that called clairvoyance?" Janet asked Hallie. "When you think of something, or dream about it, and then it happens?"

"I think so. I watched a TV show about it once." Hallie trotted along beside Janet. They were at the end of the block now. To their right, there was a break in the fence. Through that break, a path led down into the arroyo. "My brother thinks it's all baloney, but I know my mom kind of believes in it. She says time isn't a straight line, but a circle."

"I don't get it," Janet said. "Does that mean we come back around and do the same things all over again?"

"Like Mrs. Miller's algebra class? I sure hope not."

Janet led the way down the path. Soon she and Hallie were stumbling down into the arroyo, skidding on fallen leaves and gravel. "Be careful," she said. "This was so much easier last night when Storm took me."

Hallie laughed. "I bet. Where to now?"

"We have to cross the creek," Janet explained when they were on its banks.

"Wow. I've never crossed the creek before." From the expression in her wide blue eyes, Janet could tell that Hallie was starting to lose her nerve.

"It's okay," Janet assured her. "There's nothing to be afraid of."

"I don't know about that, Marshall. Last night you were dreaming, and now it's real," Hallie said. "Aren't there supposed to be rattlesnakes and mountain lions on the other side?" she asked. "We're not supposed to go over there, remember?"

"That's where Storm went," Janet insisted. "We'll never find her if we don't cross the stream."

"Okay, okay," Hallie said reluctantly. "But if anything happens to me, it's all your fault. And just remember, I am my mother's favorite—and only—daughter."

Janet laughed. "Nothing's going to happen to you. I promise."

Janet led the way to the creek. The stream seemed a lot higher now that she was on foot than it had the night before from Storm's back. The fast-rushing water cascaded over slippery, moss-covered boulders. During a flood, the creek could be deadly. Right now, it was simply treacherous.

"Careful, Jan," Hallie warned as Janet took a step forward, looking for footing on a wide boulder. "Make sure it's solid. You don't want to put your weight down and have it move under you. Stick to the dry boulders. That way you won't fall."

"If you're so sure of yourself," Janet joked, "why aren't you going first?"

Hallie laughed. "It wasn't my dream, remember?"

Janet took her friend's advice to heart. The streets of San Francisco weren't exactly good preparation for crossing creeks, even in hiking boots. She found a solid, dry boulder and stepped onto it from the bank of the creek. Then she spotted another, just a foot away. Stepping carefully from one rock to the next, she managed to cross the creek.

When she got to the other side, Janet saw that Hallie was still on the creek bank and that she hadn't even taken her first step. "What's wrong?" she asked.

"Nothing," Hallie said. "Which rock did you start on again?"

"Weren't you watching?"

"Not carefully enough, I guess."

Janet directed her friend to the trail of boulders she'd used to cross the creek. But somehow Hallie got hung up, whereas Janet had been able to cross pretty easily.

Hallie got stuck with both her feet on one small boulder. She was looking at the next rock as if it were impossibly far away.

"Come on, Hallie," Janet urged. "You can make it."

"I'm not so sure." Hallie was chewing her gum furiously. "Maybe I should turn back and start again?"

A large cloud crossed the sky, making the sun momentarily disappear. Janet shivered. "I'll help you," she said. "Here. Hold on to me." She reached for Hallie's hand and held her up as she made the big jump to the next boulder. Then Janet backed up, guiding Hallie with her. "Got it?" she asked. Hallie nodded, concentrating hard now. "Okay," said Janet. "One more."

Janet took the last step back. One more, and she'd be on the creek bank. She was about to make her move when Hallie slipped on her boulder. Janet tried to hold her up, but Hallie teetered, then wobbled, then totally lost her balance.

"Janet!" Hallie cried.

Janet watched in horror as her friend slipped into the creek. "Hold on, Hallie," she cried. "I'm coming."

Hallie tumbled downstream, bouncing off one rock after the other. Janet rushed up onto the creek bank, following her along. "Grab on to something," she urged. "Something to stop you!"

Hallie's head disappeared underwater. She came up sputtering a moment later. Janet saw her rush toward a fallen tree branch. "There!" she cried. "Grab that branch."

But it was too late. Hallie was already past the branch. Janet felt her pulse race. *Quick, Marshall*, she told herself. *Think of something!*

Up ahead, the creek was blocked off for flood control. Just before the cement canal started, there was a huge waterfall where the creek ended and the flood control channel began.

Hallie struggled to hold herself up and take control of the ride. Janet watched her toss and turn in the water, reaching out for something—anything—to stop her fall. Finally, Janet spotted a thick tree branch on the path up ahead. She grabbed it and dragged it to the creek bank.

"Try to swim toward me," Janet yelled. "You can make it!"

Hallie seemed to understand Janet's plan. As best she could, she swam toward Janet, the branch, and the creek bank. Janet rushed down the bank and leaned over into the stream as far as she could without losing her balance. She planted her legs in the mud of the creek bank, held out the branch, and waited.

Hallie was closer. Janet held her breath. The branch might just do the job. When Hallie was within ten feet, Janet held the branch out, steeling herself for the impact.

Janet had a bird's-eye view of Hallie's horrified expression as she came racing toward the branch. Hallie held out both her hands, reached for the branch, and grabbed it.

She collided with the branch so quickly that Janet nearly dropped it. But she kept her arms stiff and didn't let go. "I got you!" she cried. "I got you."

Janet's heart was pounding as she hauled Hallie onto the creek bank. Hallie was breathless and exhausted. But she was alive.

"Wow," she said, once she'd caught her breath. "Excitement, huh?"

"Most definitely," Janet agreed. "Are you okay?"

"I'm fine," said Hallie. "I mean, I think I'm okay. A little wet, but otherwise okay. Sorry, Jan," she added, shivering in her cold clothes. "I guess I blew it, huh?"

"Don't be stupid," Janet said. "I'm the one who let you fall into the creek."

"Now that I think about it, I guess you were," Hallie said.

The clouds had thickened, and Janet could see that Hallie was shivering badly. They had to get her home and into dry clothes, or else she'd catch a bad cold. Her gaze traveled upstream, to the trails Storm had taken her on. Were they real? Was the horse back there somewhere? More than anything, she wanted to go on. But she couldn't leave Hallie here alone, and she couldn't expect her to get back by herself either. With a quiet sigh, she reached down to give her friend a hand up.

"Feel up for another crossing?" she asked. "It looks like there's only one way back, and that's the way we came."

Hallie got to her feet and managed a wan smile. "I have just one word for this whole experience, Marshall."

"Let me guess," Janet said. "Excitement, right?"

"Nope." Hallie shook her head. "I was thinking *nightmare*."

CHAPTER FOUR

An hour later, Janet crept along the path toward the creek, alone this time. In the dark, the noises coming from the woods sounded like bears, instead of squirrels or birds. She turned every step or so to look over her shoulder. As if she could see a snake in the dark!

It was almost five, and the sun was starting to set. The fact that it was getting dark didn't make her feel any better. Sure, she had a flashlight, but that didn't do much good. The creek was a lot darker and colder than she remembered it, and the boulders a lot harder to find.

She hadn't told anyone—not even Hallie—that she was coming back. Given what she knew about the arroyo, it was probably a stupid plan to come here by herself, but Janet couldn't stop herself. She was determined to search for Storm. By now, all she could think of was the beautiful white mare and how incredible it would be to ride her again. She didn't want to wait for the night, to find out if Storm would come to her in her dream again, or tomorrow, when Hallie might be able to go with her again. The arroyo was like a magnet, luring her back.

On Storm, the trip across the creek and up into the canyon lands had seemed short and easy. On foot, it was a lot longer—and a lot harder. The high sagebrush scraped at her arms, and the way up was steep. By the time she got to the canyon walls, Janet was panting and beginning to wonder if maybe she should turn back.

But then she heard the sound of the waterfall in the distance. Even in the dark, Janet could see the shadowy outlines of the bats and the caves where they lived.

Just like my dream, she thought.

How could she have imagined this? Every detail felt the same. Even the path that led away from the canyon walls was lined with the same grove of sycamores. The scene was so familiar, she was scared to even think about what it could mean.

In the dark, her heart sounded almost as loud as the noises around her. As she got closer to the overgrown path where Storm had disappeared, she began to wonder what she'd find there. If all this was the same, was it possible that Storm could be real, too? It seemed like the only explanation. After all, she'd never explored this part of the arroyo before. She had no way of knowing what it looked like or if there were waterfalls and bats. Maybe she really *had* been clairvoyant.

Up ahead, Janet spotted the same old oak, fallen across the trail. She drew in another sharp breath. As she climbed over the oak, she remembered Storm's soaring jump over the tree trunk. If Storm really was real, and if Janet really did find her, they would make an incredible pair, winning ribbons all over the state. Janet Marshall riding Storm—they'd go to the regionals, then on to the championships at Madison Square Garden. After that, maybe even to the Olympics…

She kept her eyes peeled for the overgrown path. The wild thicket was on her left. The trail where Storm had left her couldn't be far.

Then, in the exact same spot as in her dream, Janet found the small opening in the sagebrush. She looked down to see if there were hoofprints in the dusty trail from the night before.

Sure enough, there they were: a set of four prints, left by a horse.

Faced with the path, Janet hesitated. A strange feeling came over her, one that made the hair stand up on the back of her neck. At first, she thought it was the wind. But the leaves on the trees were motionless. She listened. An animal maybe? But the woods were silent. If anything, the spot was too quiet, too empty.

Janet stood still and listened. She heard it distinctly—a hum in the air, one that felt as if it went through her body. In a movie, the hum might sound eerie, but for some reason she wasn't afraid. If anything, the hum made her feel excited. When she stepped closer to the path, the hum got louder. Now it felt as if her whole body was tingling. She shivered.

Pushing aside the wild sagebrush, she stepped onto the path. The woods were so thick, Janet didn't have time to think about the fact that they might be scary, too. She peeled back the branches, going slowly down the trail. All the while, the hum was still there. The farther she went, the more excited she got.

At the end of the trail, her heart stopped.

In the middle of a wide clearing, she saw a ranch. There was a corral, a barn, and a main building. Someone had slung a saddle over a rail of the corral. And there was smoke coming from the chimney of the ranch house.

Janet took a few careful steps forward. For some reason, she still wasn't afraid. Somehow, she knew she'd found Storm's home. She could only think about seeing the horse again. She walked through the corral and toward the barn. From inside, she heard the sound of animals braying softly. She peered through a crack in the barn wall and saw a cow and a pig in their stalls. Farm tools hung from hooks along the walls. There were beds of straw in the horse stalls and feed in the buckets.

"Storm," Janet whispered.

Since the horse wasn't in her stall, Janet decided to explore some more. On the porch of the ranch house, she peered inside. There was a small table, set for dinner. Steam came from a pot on the stove. Janet's stomach rumbled at the smell of dinner cooking.

"Can I help you?" a voice called out.

Janet spun on her heels, startled. Her heart pounded in her chest as she looked around, not sure what to expect. She was trespassing, and whoever lived here might not be happy about the idea.

"You looking for something?"

The voice belonged to a young boy. A very cute boy, Janet noticed, who looked about fifteen. He was standing by the corral, staring at her. His curly dark hair had straw in it, and his denim shirt was covered in dust. He slapped his jeans to raise more dust, continuing to look at Janet with a quizzical expression.

"I—I—I'm sorry for disturbing you," Janet said. "But I was looking for a horse."

"What kind of horse?" the boy asked.

"She's all white, with a gray mane and black eyes," Janet said. "I think she might be Arabian, but I'm not sure."

"I take it this isn't your horse, then?" the boy said.

"No. Why?"

"Because you don't know what kind she is."

Janet stuck out her jaw. "I know what she looks like. Isn't that enough?"

The boy raised an eyebrow. "Not enough to prove she's yours. If'n I'd seen her, which I haven't."

A wind rustled through the oaks overhead, and Janet saw the darkened shape of a hawk in the deepening light. She turned back to the boy, puzzled. "I kind of tracked her here," she said.

"How long have you been missing this horse?" the boy asked. "And what made you come out here looking for her? How did you find this place anyway?"

Janet avoided his question. "The truth is, I'm not missing her," she said. "Well, not exactly."

"So she *isn't* yours."

Janet and the boy stared at one another.

"No," Janet admitted. "She isn't mine. I'm trying to find her for a friend," she lied. More than anything, she didn't want to go without finding out if Storm really lived here. But for some reason, the boy wasn't being much help.

"Huh. Well, why don't you tell me your name and if'n I find her, I'll be sure to let you know."

"My name's Janet," she said. "Janet Marshall. What's yours?"

The boy hesitated. "John," he said finally. "John Grady. But everyone calls me J.G."

"Well, J.G., if you do see the horse, can you please give me a call? My number's listed."

"Number?" J.G. said.

"Telephone number," said Janet.

"Oh," J.G. said. "Oh, yeah, right. We kind of live simply out here," he said. "Don't have a telephone. A lot of us out here don't have them yet. Kinda inconvenient to run the wires, if you know what I mean."

Janet was disappointed. "So how will I know if you

find the horse?" she asked. "Can I come back?"

J.G. looked over his shoulder. "I really don't think I'll be finding her," he said. "And I'd really rather you didn't come back, Janet. No offense, but we don't take too well to visitors. That's why we live back here. We kind of like the silence, if you know what I mean. So if you don't mind, I think you'd better be leaving now, all right?"

"Okay," Janet said. "I'm sorry I bothered you."

She turned to go, disappointed and frustrated. She felt sure that Storm had led her to the path because the ranch was important. For some reason, the horse wanted Janet to find her. Why else had she turned up in her dreams?

As she walked away, Janet was aware of J.G.'s eyes on her back, watching her leave. Obviously, he meant it when he said they didn't take to visitors. Was there a reason he didn't want her to find the horse? What if Storm didn't live here? What if she was actually stolen? Maybe J.G. knew that if Janet discovered Storm, she would ask questions about her, possibly even take her away.

J.G. was hiding something—Janet was sure of it. And she wasn't going to leave until she found out what.

When she got to the trailhead, she stopped. After waiting a few minutes, she crept back up the path, careful to hide in the shadow of the sycamore trees. She got to a spot where she could see the ranch. And then she waited.

J.G. lifted the saddle off the corral rail and disappeared inside the barn. Then he came back out to the corral and finished clearing it up, putting away the leads and bridles that were tossed around. When he was done, he stepped onto the porch and went inside. He was gone for a while. Janet became aware of the time passing and the rumblings in her stomach. Maybe she was wrong. Maybe J.G. didn't know anything about Storm. But why did Storm lead her here last night, then?

She was just about to give up when J.G. came back outside to the porch and began to ring a dinner bell there. And that's when Janet's suspicions paid off.

A blur of white came streaking down from the hills behind the house. It was Storm!

Janet held her breath.

Storm raced up to the porch. J.G. reached out to pet her nose. The animal nuzzled J.G.'s hand, obviously playing with a friend.

"So you've never seen her, huh?" Janet mumbled under her breath. Clearly, Storm lived at the ranch, and clearly, she knew J.G. The boy was putting a bridle and lead on her now and taking her back to the stables. Even from a distance, Janet could hear him speaking to the animal in low, affectionate terms. He patted her on the side as they went, stroking her glowing white coat.

Before J.G. had a chance to disappear, Janet raced up the path. As she came into the clearing, J.G. stopped short. Both he and Storm looked at Janet in surprise.

"You thought I left, didn't you?" Janet guessed. "Well, I didn't. Don't ask me why, but I had a feeling you were hiding something. So I guess the question is, why? Why didn't you tell me about Storm? All you had to say was that she was your horse."

J.G. bit on the inside of his mouth, obviously trying to come up with an explanation. "The truth is, Janet, this is my older sister's horse. We call her Lady. Sometimes she runs off and disappears, and we don't know where she's gone. I guess she's got the canyon lands in her blood, you know, wanting to roam free. But no one ever comes looking for her. And the fact is that my sister— her name's Larissa—well, she's got a hopping temper. I knew that if I told you the horse lived here, you'd want to hang out and see her. I also know Larissa pretty well— she's real possessive of Lady—and that just wouldn't fly. Even though she might like you, 'cause you wear jeans and all, and that's not usual for a girl. Anyway, can you blame me? I'm just trying to stay out of trouble."

Janet was still mad at him for lying to her, but J.G.'s smile was wide and winning. A curly lock of brown hair fell onto his forehead, and there was a pleading expression in his blue eyes.

Even if he weren't so cute—which he was, Janet noticed yet again—she would have had trouble resisting him, especially now that she knew that, from the start, he hadn't been mean to her so much as protective.

"No," she said. "I guess I can't."

"Did you want to say hi?" J.G. asked, patting Storm's side.

"Do I!"

As J.G. led Storm to her, she screwed her face up

47

into a smile. She didn't want him to see how disappointed she was. He'd never understand. She'd found the horse, but now she knew that Storm would never be hers. She nearly cried as the mare pranced on her long, stately legs and tossed her head as Janet reached out to pet her. "I think she remembers me," she said, looking deep into the mare's black eyes. "Don't you, girl?"

Storm nuzzled Janet's hand. With that one touch, their whole journey came flooding back to her: Storm showing up at her window, their ride through the arroyo. It was heartbreaking to think she'd never own the horse. Janet hadn't known until just that moment how much she'd been counting on it.

"J.G., do you think I could ride her?" she asked. "Just once? Before I go back?"

"I'm not so sure," J.G. said, looking over his shoulder.

"Please?" Janet begged. "Afterward, I promise I'll leave. Cross my heart."

J.G. paused. "Larissa's still up in the canyon, collecting firewood. I guess there's a little time. Let me get a saddle."

Janet held on to Storm's lead as J.G. disappeared into the barn. She spoke to the animal in low tones. "It's like I really was meant to find you," she whispered. "Wait until I tell Hallie. She'll die!"

"Here you go," said J.G., coming back with a blanket and saddle. "Lady doesn't love a tight girth, so I like to keep it loose." Janet watched as he fastened the buckles on the girth, then ran the straps under the horse and tightened them on the other side. Then he sized up Janet. "Five feet?" he asked. "Maybe five two?" When Janet nodded, he adjusted the stirrups for her size. "You're a little smaller than Larissa, so Lady will take to you like a dream. Ready?"

"You bet!" Janet stepped toward the mare, grabbed on to the reins, and put her toe in the stirrup. She cocked her foot so that it was down and pressing forward, then she lifted her right leg up and swung it around. The mount was clean and even, and Storm hardly moved an inch.

"Nice work," J.G. said appreciatively. "You ride a lot?"

"Since I was a kid," Janet said proudly. "But I don't have a horse of my own."

"You don't?" J.G. asked in disbelief. "How come?"

Janet patted Storm's side and counted off the reasons. "No room, not enough money, parents can't afford it."

"Weird," J.G. said, shaking his head. "I never heard of a girl who doesn't have a horse. Your parents don't have a ranch?"

"A ranch?" Janet laughed. "Try a ranch house."

"Huh." J.G. shook his head. "Lady's really good with the aids. You don't need to do a lot of tugging and pulling. Just a small move with the reins is enough. Don't saw the bit in her mouth or jab her with your legs."

Janet held back a smile. J.G. would just about die if she told him that she'd ridden the mare before—and bareback at that. Instead, she led the mare into the corral at an easy walk. Once they got inside, J.G. closed the gate behind them and Janet clucked Storm into a trot. Just as in her dream, Storm responded to the lightest pressure between Janet's legs. Now that the mare was on the bit, Janet was able to guide Storm easily around the corral. The slightest movement from her outside leg and the smallest pull on the inside rein had Storm making graceful turns around the corral. Soon Janet was ready to take her into a canter.

First, Janet slowed from a fast to a sitting trot. Then she sat deeper in the saddle and moved her legs farther back on Storm's barrel. "Come on, girl," she said, easing up on the reins.

Janet gave the cue. In a flash, Storm had picked up speed and was in a solid, rolling canter. Janet settled into the wavelike rhythm, enjoying the feel of Storm's strong muscles and powerful gait taking her around the ring.

"Nice moves," J.G. said. "See if you can take the jump."

In the center of the corral, there was a set of poles about a foot off the ground. Janet slowed Storm to a fast trot and made several more circles of the corral, then lined up to take the jump. She guided Storm carefully, got her balance, and prepared to set the jump. A few feet from the poles, Janet sat down in the saddle and steered and pushed with her back and seat. The secret was to get the proper impulsion so the horse would be ready for anything.

Right at the jump, Janet inclined her body forward into a nice, relaxed two point. Her shoulders settled over the mare's mane, ready to go with the horse when she jumped.

Beneath her, Storm's neck stretched for the take-off. Then she felt Storm's front legs leave the ground. For a moment, Janet's seat left the saddle, but she kept her weight on her thighs and knees and kept her balance. The horse sailed over the poles. Behind her, Janet felt Storm's hind legs leave the ground, and for a moment, they were airborne.

The jump took Janet's breath away. The horse knew exactly what to do, without Janet telling her. On the other side of the jump, Storm landed with an easy thud, while Janet sank effortlessly back into her seat.

"Beautiful!" J.G. cried. "You really do know what you're doing, huh?"

"It's Storm!" Janet was breathless with excitement. In all her riding experience, she'd never taken a jump like that before. "She could make any rider look good. Boy, oh, boy, are you some horse," she whispered to the mare. "Let's try that again."

While she led Storm around the corral, taking the jump again and again, Janet finally understood why her grandfather had always said that the best horse made you feel as if rider and beast were one. Riding Storm made her feel as if girl and mare were one.

If only she could ride Storm every day, Janet thought. Maybe even enter her in the season opener.

Was there a way to convince J.G. to let her borrow the horse? She just knew that riding Storm she'd win ribbons. She'd seen what the horse could do, and it was more than any other horse she'd ever ridden. More than Duke or MacDougal or Yankee. Riding Storm, she'd beat Hallie and Becky and all the other girls at the stables.

Janet was deep into a rolling canter—and even deeper in her fantasy—when a young woman raced into the clearing. Her eyes were wild with anger, and her mouth twisted in rage when she spotted Janet.

"What's going on here?" she shouted. "Who are you, and what on earth are you doing on my horse?"

CHAPTER FIVE

*J*anet pulled up on the horse. Storm came to a dead halt—so quickly in fact, that Janet had to stop herself from tumbling face forward off the mare.

"Larissa, take it easy," J.G. said, holding the girl back. "This is Janet. She asked if she could ride Lady."

"And you let her," Larissa said angrily. She stalked into the corral, grabbed Storm's reins, and ordered Janet to dismount. "John Grady, how could you? How could you let some strange...*girl*...ride my horse? You think I'd let someone just get on one of your prized Appaloosas and race around the corral? Not on your life you wouldn't."

So this is Larissa, Janet thought. No wonder J.G. hadn't wanted to tell Janet about the horse. J.G. had said his sister had a hopping temper, and he wasn't kidding.

With her curly dark hair and her slender build, Larissa was an even better looking version of her younger brother. Compared to Janet, who was just plain with her long brown hair, freckles, and brown eyes, Larissa was beautiful. But the girl's blue eyes blazed with anger where J.G.'s sparkled with humor and amusement. And where J.G.'s features were soft and flattering, the angles of Larissa's face made her seem like an angry bird as she moved around the corral, untacking Storm and throwing her saddle over the rails.

And even though Larissa didn't seem in the mood to listen to reason, Janet braved an apology. "I'm sorry," she said. "It wasn't his fault. It was mine. It's just that I saw Storm before—"

"Storm?" Larissa said.

"That's what I called her," Janet explained. "Because of her color, and because she rides like the wind."

"You sound like you know from experience," J.G. said with a smile. "But I only saw you canter just now around the corral." There was a pause. "Maybe you should tell me just what you know about this here horse," he said. "You never did explain how you came to find us down here, or why you were looking for her."

It occurred to her that she could—and probably should—lie. But how? What would she say? Somehow, the truth just seemed easier, even if it did make her sound crazy.

"Actually, I had a dream that she came to my house the other night and let me ride her all the way down here—down to the path, that is. I know it sounds strange," she said in a rush to explain. "You probably think I'm out of my mind. But I'm telling you the truth. I couldn't believe it myself when I came down here and saw this place for real, especially when I saw Storm. But it's true. I dreamt about your horse. I dreamt about this whole place—"

Janet didn't finish. Larissa was scowling, while J.G. scratched his head. Maybe it would have been better not to say anything, she thought. She should have just left, without the Gradys ever knowing how and why she'd found the ranch.

"What a weird dream," J.G. said finally.

"You bet it was," Janet agreed, relieved that J.G. didn't think she was insane. She was about to go on. But she saw from Larissa's expression that she didn't believe a word of her story.

"You know what I think?" she said. "I think you're making the whole thing up."

"Why would I do that?" Janet asked.

"So you can ride Lady," Larissa said. "You probably don't even have a horse of your own, do you?"

Janet took a deep breath. Larissa's piercing blue eyes challenged her to tell the truth. "You're right," Janet admitted. "It's true I want to ride Storm. She's an incredible horse. And no, I don't have a horse of my own. I wish I did."

"Take it easy, Lar. She didn't mean any harm," J.G. said to his sister. "I was watching her the whole time."

Between Janet's apology and J.G.'s comforting tone, Larissa softened a bit. "I guess I did overreact," she said, reaching up to pet the mare's nose. "I'm pretty protective of Lady."

"I would be, too," Janet said. "If she were mine, I mean. What breed is she?"

"Part Arabian," Larissa said proudly. "But she also has some quarter horse in her. Because she likes to roam so much, J.G. thinks she's got some mustang in her too. She can be pretty high-spirited."

"I noticed," Janet said.

"Tell us more about this dream," J.G. said, scratching his head. "I'm still trying to figure it out."

"Me too." Janet laughed. Now that Larissa had cooled down, she felt better about talking to the Gradys. She started at the beginning and told them both about Storm appearing at her window, then taking her down into the arroyo.

"Since I'd never actually been on this side of the arroyo, I was pretty amazed when I got down here and saw that everything was just like in my dream. I still don't really understand what it all means."

"I know what my Aunt Carmen would say," J.G. put in. "She'd say you got in touch with the spirit world through your dreams. And that Storm guided you. Horses have that ability, you know, to pass over between the spirit world and our world—"

Larissa rolled her eyes. "J.G., stop. You're gonna scare Janet with your talk. Besides, it's all pretty silly if you ask me."

"No, it's not," J.G. said. "I was there when Aunt

Carmen had her séance. I saw her call back Mom and Dad. So don't tell me it's silly. And look at Janet here. She wouldn't have found us if it weren't for that dream she had. She'd never even seen this place, but somehow she managed to get it all right, didn't she? So how do you explain that?"

Janet was glad that J.G. believed her. In a way, J.G. was just confirming what Hallie had said and what Janet figured had to be true in some way: that Storm was a link between her dream and reality. Even so, she didn't quite know what to think about séances and spirits. Once, she and Hallie had turned off all the lights in the bathroom, lit a candle, and spun around three times while saying "Mary Worth, Mary Worth, Mary Worth" out loud. The spell was supposed to call back the spirit of John F. Kennedy, but all Janet saw was her own shadow, and all she got out of the whole experience was a serious case of the willies. She hadn't been able to sleep that night.

It was darker than ever, Janet realized suddenly. Spirits or no spirits, she was going to be seriously late if she didn't get home soon. "I've got to go," she told J.G. and Larissa. "Would it be okay if I came back? To visit Storm, I mean."

J.G. and Larissa exchanged a look. Janet could tell that J.G. was willing but that Larissa still wasn't sure. "Come on, Lar," J.G. said. "There's no one else around here our age. Uncle Cal wouldn't mind."

Larissa hesitated. "When Uncle Cal went up to Santa

Barbara to see after the other farm, he left us in charge, remember? You're not going to ditch your chores every time she comes around, are you?"

"I won't," J.G. said. "I promise."

"Okay," Larissa said. "But only Janet. I don't want a million of her friends tagging along. We *do* have a ranch to run, in case you've forgotten."

With that, Larissa said a quick good-bye to Janet, clucked at Storm, and led her back to the stables. Once she was gone, J.G. leaned over and whispered to Janet, "See? She's not all bad. Maybe if you stick on her good side, she'll let you ride Storm again."

Janet smiled to herself, happy to hear J.G. call the mare Storm instead of Lady.

"And if she doesn't," J.G. said, "we can always sneak in a ride or two." He winked. "But that's just between you and me, okay?"

Back home, the lights were on and both cars were in the driveway. Another car was parked out front, and Janet could hear a booming laugh coming from inside the house.

Leonard! She'd completely forgotten that her father's boss was coming over for dinner. Her mother was going to kill her! Correction, Janet thought, looking down at her dirty, creek-soaked clothes. First she'd kill her, and then she'd serve her head on a platter.

The hall clock chimed seven as Janet tried to sneak upstairs.

"Not so fast," came her father's voice. "Where have you been?" Her dad appeared in the doorway to the living room. He took one look at her and said, "And what on earth have you been doing? Janet! Answer me."

There was no point in lying now, at least not about all of it. "Dad, I'm sorry. Hallie and I went down into the arroyo. Then Hallie fell in, and I had to save her, and I've been at her house since then, making sure she's okay."

"The arroyo! You know you're supposed to stay out of there," her father said.

"I know, I know. It's just that we really felt like exploring and it seemed like it would be okay," Janet said.

"What seemed like it would be okay?" her mother asked. "Janet! Look at you! What happened?"

"She fell into the creek," her father explained.

"Not me, Dad. Hallie. But I saved her."

Her mother let out a long sigh. "I am not even going to ask. Just go upstairs and get cleaned up," she said. "We're eating in five minutes."

Janet knew she should feel bad about being late—and lying to her parents. But all during dinner she couldn't stop thinking about the ranch, and Larissa and J.G., and, most of all, Storm. She couldn't wait to tell Hallie!

Then she remembered she'd promised J.G. that only she would come to the ranch. That meant she really couldn't tell Hallie, or else Hallie would want to come, too. She would have to lie to her friend as well as to her parents. It was all getting so complicated!

"Earth to Janet," Mr. Marshall was saying. "Come in, Janet. Vanilla or chocolate ice cream on your pie?"

"Huh?" Janet looked up and saw all three grownups staring at her. "Oh, vanilla. Sorry, Dad. I wasn't listening."

"No kidding," Leonard said. "You were a million miles away just now. Want to tell us where?"

"Nowhere," Janet said. "Dad, do you think anyone actually lives down in the arroyo?" she asked. "I mean, like ranchers and stuff?"

"Not that I know of. Leonard, what do you think?"

Her father's boss swallowed a big bite of pie. "Used to, a long time ago," he said. "I think I remember seeing an article about it in the *Times* when I first started working there. But don't forget that's a flood zone. No one's allowed to build down there now. Great pie, if I do say so myself."

Her mother smiled. This was Leonard's classic line. He always brought the pie, and he always complimented it. "Why do you ask?" he said.

"I don't know," Janet said with a shrug. "Just wondering, I guess."

"Well, it's been undeveloped for as long as I've lived here," Leonard said. "And that's going on twenty years now. But it would make for an interesting piece in the *Times,*" he said. "Don't think we've done much about the history down there in a while." He pushed his chair back from the table and stood up. "Sorry, Liz, but I've got to run. It was great, as usual. Thanks."

While her parents saw Leonard to the door, Janet sat staring at her melted ice cream. If what Leonard was true, then it didn't really make sense that the ranch had been able to survive. Unless no one knew about it, which was possible, considering how deep in the arroyo she'd had to go to find it. Janet smiled to herself. Before, it felt weird to keep the ranch a secret. Now she was getting used to the idea. In fact, she liked knowing something no one else knew. She could go there, to her secret place, and no one would know where she was.

When Janet's parents came back into the kitchen, the smiles were gone. "Your mother and I are very upset about this afternoon," her father said. "You or Hallie could have been seriously hurt."

"I know, Dad, and I'm really sorry. It won't happen again."

"No, it won't," her mother went on. "Because from now on, unless you're at the stables, you're coming home straight after school."

"But Mom—"

"Don't 'but Mom' me," her mother said. "You disobeyed us, Janet. We're not going to take away your job. But other than that, you can consider yourself grounded."

"Grounded?" It was too much. First Yankee, now this. Janet felt her face flush with anger. "But Hallie's birthday party is this weekend," she said. "Everyone's going!"

"Everyone except you," her father said. "I'm sorry,

Janet. I know it may seem harsh, but how else will you learn to mind what we say? We told you that the arroyo is dangerous, and you went down there anyway. Your mother and I both work, so we can't be here to make sure you listen to everything we say. This is the only alternative. Sorry, Janet. For the next month, you're sticking close to home. And that's that."

Grounded?

For a month?

It was unreal. How would she get back to the ranch? If she went down into the arroyo, she'd be lying to her parents all over again. And if they found out she was lying to them, she could get grounded for life.

Janet was still thinking about how to get around it when she got to school the next day. She hardly noticed the group of girls standing in front of her locker.

"It was amazing, Janet, wasn't it?" Hallie was saying. "Tell them. Tell them about how I almost went over the falls."

Janet looked up and recognized Cody, with her curly brown hair, and Becky, and Aloe. "It's true," she said with a nod. "She was this close to going over. You should have heard her scream!"

"Janet!" Hallie protested. "I did not scream!"

"You bet you did," Janet said. Telling about their adventure was almost taking her mind off being grounded. Almost. "You were screaming harder than if you were on the roller coaster at Magic Mountain. And when you got out of the water—phew! Good thing Garrett didn't see you then."

Garrett was a guy in ninth grade Hallie had an incredible crush on. Aloe laughed and tossed back her ponytail. "So are you going back? You know, to look for that horse?" she asked.

"I don't know," Hallie said, still smiling. "Are we, Janet?"

That's when Janet realized what must have happened: Hallie had told them—about Storm, the dream, everything. After promising that she wouldn't. She shot Hallie an icy look. "What horse?" she asked.

"The horse in your dream," Becky said smugly, holding her books to her chest. "The one you were looking for."

"Sorry, Jan," Hallie whispered under her breath. "I guess it slipped out."

"Sounds like," Janet said. All her misery came flooding back. No visits to the arroyo, no rides on Storm. No party at Hallie's, even though after what she'd just found out, she wasn't sure she wanted to go anyway. "The truth is, I'm not going anywhere. My parents grounded me last night. For the next month, I have to be at home or at the stables—no in between."

"What about my party?" Hallie asked.

Janet shook her head.

"Jan!" Hallie wailed. "It's going to be so cool. I can't

believe your parents aren't going to let you come."

"Well, they're not. Listen, Hallie, I gotta go. See you later."

Janet walked off, feeling about thirty times worse than the night before. She couldn't believe Hallie had spilled the beans about her dream. Now all the girls knew why she and Hallie had been in the arroyo, and there was no telling who else might go exploring there. She'd felt bad before about not telling Hallie that she'd actually found Storm, but not anymore. Instead, she made a pact with herself right then and there never to tell her friend another thing, not as long as she lived.

"Hey, Jan," Hallie called out. "Wait up."

There was no way to avoid Hallie, even though Janet wished she could. They were both on their way to algebra. After that, they had history together. She was going to have to look at Hallie all morning, whether she liked it or not.

"Listen, I'm really sorry," Hallie said. "I know I wasn't supposed to tell. I guess I just got carried away when I was telling my story."

"I guess so," Janet said, walking fast.

"So we're really not going back, huh?" Hallie said. "I guess I blew it."

"Kind of," Janet agreed.

Hallie grabbed on to Janet's arm. "Jan, come on. You're not going to be mad at me forever, are you?"

Janet turned to face her friend. Of all the people she'd met in her new school and her new neighborhood, she liked Hallie the most. But right now, she was too mad to say anything.

Hallie's blue eyes were wide with worry. She seemed to realize Janet wasn't going to forgive her immediately, because she stiffened and her eyes narrowed. "Okay, Jan," she said. "I thought we were friends, but I guess we're not. Because right now if you were my friend, you'd say what I did was okay."

With that, Hallie walked away. Janet watched her go. Somehow, she just couldn't find the words to call her back.

CHAPTER SIX

There were two paths before Janet: one led home, the other to the ranch. Her chores at the stables were done. Her parents wouldn't be home until six.

You promised them, Marshall, a voice said.

But they don't have to know, she argued back.

They'll know, the voice said. *They know everything.*

Janet knew that what she was doing was wrong, but it felt as if the trail down into the arroyo was calling out her name. Hallie wasn't talking to her. Aloe and Cody and Becky were ignoring her, too. What was she supposed to do, head home and watch old reruns on TV?

Twenty minutes later, she was across the creek, heading for the ranch. The moment she reached the hidden path, the one that led to the ranch, she felt the same energy she had the day before, the same tingling feeling that something truly incredible could happen. No wonder she couldn't resist coming here. Just getting close to the ranch made her feel fifty times better. Up ahead, a warm afternoon light shone down on the clearing, casting a soft glow on the corral, barn, and ranch house.

"Hey, kiddo," J.G. said when he spotted her. He was fixing rails on the corral, nailing them back onto their posts. "I didn't expect you back so soon. What's wrong? You look kind of glum."

Janet climbed up to sit on top of the corral. She swung her legs under her, catching them on the rails. If she had been glum before, she didn't feel that way now. "Nothing," she said.

"Doesn't look like nothing," J.G. said. There was that smile again, Janet thought. She had to admit that her heart beat a little faster when she was around J.G. And why shouldn't it? He was an older guy and utterly cute. "So why don't you tell me what's what?"

"Let's see," Janet said. "I had a huge fight with my best friend, and my parents grounded me last night. Otherwise, everything's great."

"Grounded?" J.G. stopped hammering and looked up at Janet, confused. "I'm not sure I know what you mean."

Janet laughed. "What? You mean you've never been grounded before? Everyone gets grounded!"

"Not that I know of," J.G. laughed. "We live kind of backward down here, in case you haven't noticed."

"No kidding. Well, grounded basically means that I can't go anywhere or do anything for the next month unless my parents say it's okay."

"How come?" J.G. asked.

Janet hesitated. "Are you sure you want to hear this?" she asked. "I mean, it can't be very interesting to you."

"Sure it is," J.G. said. "Go on, tell me what you did."

"Okay," Janet said. She felt a little self-conscious talking about herself to J.G., who was a guy after all, but she did her best. "My friend Hallie and I aren't supposed to come down into the arroyo. But we did anyway, and Hallie fell into the creek, and she almost went over the falls, and my mom and dad found out, and now I'm not supposed to be anywhere but home and the stables. Period. And I told Hallie not to let anyone know what we'd done or where we were going since I wanted it to be a secret, in case we did find the ranch, and she told all the girls at school, so now I'm mad at her."

"Whew." J.G. wiped the sweat from his forehead with his shirt sleeve. "You do have problems. What happens if your parents find out you've been down here? They don't know you're coming here, do they?" he guessed.

"Not exactly." Janet waited to see how J.G. would react. "But they don't have to find out, do they? I mean, if it's still okay for me to come, that is."

"Well—" J.G. dragged out the word, and Janet felt her heart stop. Was he going to tell her that he'd changed his mind? He hadn't seemed upset to see her when she showed up. "Hey, relax!" he added, laughing. "I was just pulling your leg. Sure, it's okay for you to come. Larissa's only eighteen, but she acts like the boss when my aunt and uncle are away. I know it seems she's against it, but personally, I like the company. And to tell you the truth, I kind of enjoy getting under her skin a little bit. She's a lot like the way our dad used to be. She could use a little loosening up."

Janet could hear the sadness in J.G.'s voice. "What happened to your parents?" she asked.

"Ranching accident," J.G. said in a flat tone. "It happens. There was flooding in the arroyo and they went to save some cattle."

"That's terrible," Janet said. J.G. seemed so calm about it. Could it really be that easy to get over your parents' death? She doubted it. "What happened?"

"They got swept away by the current," J.G. explained. "Them and the cattle both. Listen, Janet, if you don't mind, I'd rather not talk about it. That's ranching. It's dangerous, and you have to deal with what happens. Nothing I can say or do now can bring them back, as much as I wish that weren't the case."

"I understand," Janet said. "I'm sorry."

J.G. gave her a thin smile. "It's okay."

"My dad's boss told me this is a flood zone," Janet said. "Supposedly, no one can build down here."

J.G. raised an eyebrow. "Is that so? I guess my dad didn't know about it." He smiled. "Then again, he wasn't much of a rancher. He got this land cheap—I suppose that's why—and every winter he fought the creek. One year, it just got the better of him. We keep the cattle away from the creek, and otherwise we stick to simple farming. Want to see the ranch?"

"You bet I do!" Janet said.

Janet had spent a lot of time in the country, roaming the land around her grandparents' ranch, but she'd never seen any spot as beautiful as the Gradys' spread. Behind the ranch house, a steep trail went up to the canyon. There, another branch of the creek cut through the land, running alongside the canyon and putting their ranch lands between two forks of the same mountain stream. North of the barn, the land spread out into a wide open meadow. Next to it there were several fields. One was sown with hay for the livestock. Another had rows and rows of vegetables. A third was where the cattle grazed. Thick groves of sycamores shielded the fields from the rest of the arroyo. The whole place was set miles back from the trail that went along the creek. Unless you knew about the ranch, you could easily miss it.

"We pretty much live off the land," J.G. said, once they were out on the back pasture, looking up at the mountains. "It's a hard life, but we love it."

So did Janet. As far as the eye could see, there were rolling hills and groves of sycamore and oak. Her neighborhood, the freeways, all that hustle and bustle felt a million miles away. In the distance, the mountains rose, deep blue and majestic.

"It's like magic," she said with a sigh.

"I know what you mean," J.G. agreed. "Well, from the sun I'd say it's time to get back. You don't want your parents coming home before you now, do you?"

Back at the ranch, Larissa was coming out of the barn just as J.G. and Janet walked up. She seemed surprised to see Janet, but this time she actually gave her a smile and a hello. "Sorry about yesterday," she said. "It was a little dumb of me to jump down your throat like that."

"That's okay," Janet said. "I should have asked permission before I rode Storm—I mean, Lady. I'm the one who's sorry."

"Well, I accept your apology." Larissa set down the bucket of milk she was carrying. "In the meantime, I've been thinking." She paused for a moment and rested her hand on her slender hip. Without the anger in her voice and her expression, Larissa really was beautiful. "Sometimes Lady goes all day without exercise, if I don't go out to the fields," Larissa went on. "So if you do want to come down and ride her, I suppose I wouldn't mind. You just have to promise to be careful. She may look like she could race a marathon, but she's been known to get sick from time to time. Be careful about letting her graze, and don't let her eat anything but the timothy and oats from the barn. Otherwise, just take it easy on her, okay?"

Janet could hardly contain her delight. "Okay," she said. "I promise. Oh, Larissa, thank you. You don't know what this means to me."

Larissa gave Janet a wide, genuine smile. "I think I do," she said. "There was a time when I didn't have my own horse either, and I remember how it felt. A friend of my father's let me ride his Appaloosa. I was so happy, I went over to his ranch almost every day. Finally, he got so tired of seeing me, he decided to give me the horse."

"That's a true story," J.G. said with a laugh. "Seems like you two have a lot in common."

"How do you mean?" Janet asked, not sure how she could possibly have much in common with Larissa, who was tall, stately, and beautiful. Not to mention about five years older.

"I mean, you're both as stubborn as mules," J.G. said. "When it comes to horses, that is."

Stubborn is right, Janet thought as she coaxed Sugar into the practice ring a few days later. So stubborn that she still hadn't made up with Hallie. So stubborn that when Connie offered to let her ride Sugar in the season opener, she had to be convinced it was the best she'd be able to do. All that mattered to her right now was Storm, and riding her, and hanging out with J.G. So what if that meant she didn't have any friends?

"Come on," Janet said, dragging the school horse forward on his bridle. "I'm not enjoying this any more than you are."

The truth was, if she could have anything in the world, it would be the chance to train Storm. But that wasn't going to happen. And since Janet had no plans to give up riding in the season opener, she was stuck with Sugar, whether she liked it or not.

Connie had said to keep things simple with the gelding. He probably wouldn't win her a blue ribbon, but he could place well in all three events. For now, Janet had decided to concentrate on eq, since this was where she had the hardest time. She tended to pull the bit when a horse didn't cooperate, and tug a little on the reins. Also, on a slowpoke like Sugar, Janet lost her concentration if the horse didn't respond immediately to her moves. All these factors made training on Sugar difficult.

"Just an hour," Janet said. "That's all I'm asking for today."

The problem was that Sugar got worked all day. By the time her turn came, the horse didn't want to budge. Today was no exception. Janet had no sooner mounted than Sugar got it into his head to head for the gate and home.

"Sorry, kiddo," Janet told him. "Not so fast."

Hallie was already in the practice ring, working with her horse, Duke. Connie sat on the bleachers to the side, ready to give Janet feedback and instruction. Janet took a few turns, warming up Sugar. Each time she passed Hallie, the girl looked the other way. Since she knew she wouldn't be able to train with this sort of distraction, Janet decided to make the first move. She rode up to Hallie and trotted alongside.

"Hi," she said.

Hallie's eyes under her riding hat stayed fixed ahead.

"I heard you're going out with Garrett," Janet said. The eighth-grade gossip mill hadn't stopped running just because Janet wasn't part of it. She knew about Hallie's party that weekend, and that she and Garrett had ended up making out. "That's great. You must be really happy."

Hallie's eyes narrowed. She sure didn't look happy.

"Well, that's all I wanted to say. Take it easy."

Janet rode off. What a waste that had been, she thought. Sure, maybe if she actually apologized for getting mad at her, Hallie might have had two words to say. But wasn't it also Hallie's fault they weren't talking to one another? Hallie had been the one to tell Becky and the other girls about looking for Storm, after promising Janet that she wouldn't. So whose fault was it, really?

Janet gave up thinking about it. For the next hour, she forced herself to concentrate on Sugar. From the side, Connie called out commands: back up; figure eight at a trot; figure eight at a canter; change leads; halt. Janet went through the moves as best she could, but the truth was that Sugar probably had the worst feet of any horse she'd ever ridden. Just thinking about how hard it would be to get him to do the moves perfectly made Janet freeze. She lost her concentration, slouched in her seat, and pulled back hard on the reins when it came time to make a move. Since she would be judged on the effortlessness of the moves, Janet knew she wasn't doing very well. All her cues showed, and every reaction to one of Sugar's bad steps was written on her face.

When the lesson was over, Janet dismounted and led Sugar over to Connie so they could talk. "Sorry," Janet said under her breath. They both knew the workout had been awful.

Connie shook her head. For once, she didn't even smile. "Janet, I know you're better at the moves than that. What's going on?"

"Sugar has the worst feet," Janet said, trying to blame it on the horse.

"When it comes to eq, it's up to the rider to do the job," Connie reminded her. "You weren't concentrating. I don't care how hard it is to get Sugar to do the moves, you have to look good. You know that."

"I know." Janet had made the first—and worst—rider's mistake: blaming the horse for her own faults. Especially in eq. Connie was right. It was up to Janet. And even if Sugar didn't make it easy because of his clumsy feet and awkward moves, she wasn't supposed to let that get to her.

"You can't expect to win a ribbon at the season opener if you don't take your training seriously. Let's try it again tomorrow," Connie said, getting up from the bleachers. "Go home and take it easy. You've still got some time left."

On her way out, Janet watched Hallie perform the same moves. On Duke, who was a real horse, Hallie's eq looked impressive. There was no way Janet would ever have the same form. Not on Sugar anyway. *What a lame horse,* Janet thought for the millionth time as she untacked the gelding, put away his saddle and bridle, and curried him. She knew it wasn't fair to dislike Sugar, but the truth was, his best years were over. And despite what Connie had to say, Janet didn't see how she could possibly win any ribbons on him.

It was late by the time Janet had Sugar back in his stall, but she raced down to the ranch anyway. Riding Sugar had made her even more lonesome for Storm.

When she got to the ranch, J.G. and Larissa were nowhere in sight. Janet headed into the barn, quickly saddled Storm, and led her to the corral. She didn't have time today to take Storm out on a hard gallop through the fields, but even a simple canter in the corral would take the bad taste of training Sugar out of her mouth.

She trotted around the corral, posting easily. Storm's long, graceful legs and the near-perfect sway to her back were a joy after Sugar. After cantering for a while and letting Storm get rid of some restless energy, Janet decided to try the same moves she'd been doing on Sugar.

First came the figure eights. After just a bit of coaxing, Storm took her cues and figured out how to switch lead on the diagonal. Picking up to a canter, Janet thought Storm might lose the pace. Not a chance. The mare stumbled once as she tried to figure out what Janet wanted, but after Janet pulled up and made her do it again, Storm got the knack.

And Janet noticed something else: With Storm under her, she sat higher in the seat and went through the paces with confidence. No awkward steps, no false moves. She kept erect and concentrated on her form. Storm took each step gracefully, seeming to know instinctively what Janet meant by her cues. It was a dream.

Before, Janet hadn't let herself think too much about riding Storm in the season opener. She knew what a dream it would be, but she also knew it was impossible. There was no way Larissa would let her. She was already incredibly protective of her horse. What were the odds she'd let Janet take the mare out of the arroyo and ride her in a show? *Less than zero,* Janet told herself, pushing the thought away. *Give it up, Marshall. Sugar's the only horse in your future.*

Even so, what did it hurt to see what the mare could do? She could still dream, couldn't she?

Janet was working on another figure eight at a gallop when Larissa came walking up to the corral. Her jeans were dirty, and her hair was coming out of its braid. She looked exhausted.

"What are you doing?" she asked Janet.

"Nothing," Janet said, pulling the horse to a halt. "Just an experiment."

"In what?" Larissa wanted to know.

Janet didn't answer.

"You were trying to train her, weren't you?" Larissa said.

Janet blushed. "No!" she protested. There was no way Larissa could read her mind. "It's just that I was practicing my eq earlier today on a horse at the stables, and it was a disaster. I just wanted to see how it would be to try the moves on Storm."

"And how was it?" Larissa asked.

"Like a dream," she said. "Want to see?"

Larissa didn't say yes, but she didn't say no either, so Janet went ahead and showed her the moves she'd been working on. She eased Storm into a canter, then put her through the delicate moves that would make a figure eight. Again, Storm stumbled at first, but after a few tries, Janet was able to guide her through her diagonals with a smooth, sure form. When she was done, she pulled up on Storm.

"How was that?" she asked.

"Pretty impressive," Larissa acknowledged. "I didn't realize Lady had it in her. What else can she do?"

"You'd be amazed," Janet said. "I've never seen a horse take jumps like her. She could be an incredible show horse."

"She's a ranch horse," Larissa said. "She's never been shown before in her life. It's hard enough to keep her inside the ranch lands and not have her wandering who knows where. She's got the canyon lands in her blood, Janet. That horse was meant to be wild. It's one thing to put her through these moves here in the corral, but try getting her in a show ring, and she'd bolt for sure."

"You never know unless you try," Janet said.

"And you want to try," Larissa guessed.

More than anything, Janet wanted to say. "There's a

season opener coming up in February," she told Larissa, trying to go slow, to see how she'd react. "I just know that if I rode Storm, I could win a blue ribbon. It would take a lot of training. She'd have to really learn the moves. They're still a bit sloppy at this point, but I honestly think she can do it."

"Lady's never been officially trained," Larissa said, skeptical. "I had her on a lunge for a while, but she didn't like it. I don't even know how she's managing to follow your moves."

Janet patted the horse's neck. "I don't know either, but she is. I could start from scratch and teach her vocal commands, then work up to leg and rein cues. You know, train her properly. Then you'd have your very own show horse."

"Not sure we need one," Larissa said. "You've got to remember, she's never left this ranch, not in her whole life. Who knows how she'd handle a show ring with all the other horses."

"There's always a first," Janet said.

Larissa laughed in spite of herself. "I guess my brother was right," she said. "You are almost as stubborn as I am. Okay, Janet. Let's see what you can do. If anyone can turn this horse into a show girl, I'd say it was you."

CHAPTER SEVEN

ou're gonna do *what?*" J.G. asked.

"I'm going to train Storm," Janet repeated.

"To be a show horse," he said.

"Exactly."

Janet was in the barn, mucking out Storm's stall while J.G. groomed the mare in the stall next door. "I don't know, Janet," J.G. said. "That's a bit ambitious, don't you think? Besides, to tell you the truth, I never heard of a girl training a horse. Around a ranch, that's a man's job."

Janet bristled. "Well, where I'm from, girls train horses all the time. I mean, it's not that unusual. Anyway, I know Storm can learn. She already knows the moves instinctively. She's just a little green. Sometimes she can be a bit sloppy and her form isn't always the greatest, but I know that with a little time I can make it work."

"Okay," J.G. said. "But don't come crying to me when that horse bucks you for the twentieth time in a row. Right now, she's on her best behavior. As soon as you really start making her work, it's gonna be your ninety-five pounds against her twelve hundred. And I think I know who's gonna win."

Janet smiled at the joke, but inside she knew, she just knew, that J.G. had it wrong. Storm could be trained. And she was the one to do it. When J.G. was done grooming, Janet approached Storm with a bridle and placed it over her head. She never did like the bit, and this time was no different. Storm snorted and tossed her head, but Janet spoke to her in a soothing tone and the horse quickly settled down.

Storm was a natural, but since Larissa had said that the horse had never been broken properly to ride, Janet decided to start with kindergarten training. That meant putting Storm on a lunge line. Janet found a long foot rope and attached it to Storm's bridle. Then she grabbed a whip, too, since a few strategic snaps to the mare's hooves would help get the training messages across. For the necessary rewards, she also had a pocket full of carrot pieces.

Once the mare was on a lead, Janet took her out of the barn and led her to the corral. Since the mare hadn't been exercised yet that day, Janet decided to let her run on the lunge line for a while to get rid of her energy. Storm played for a few moments, then worked up to a gallop. Janet stood in the middle of the corral while Storm raced around at a clip. After several minutes, Janet was ready to get started.

"Okay, girl," she said, letting out a long sigh. "Here goes nothing."

Janet had helped her grandfather train horses before, but she'd never done it on her own. She knew some of the basic principles, though: reward the horse, vary the session, and, above all, don't go over the same thing again and again. A bored horse becomes an unruly horse.

Standing in the middle of the corral, she raised the lunge line in her left hand so that it would lead the horse. With her right hand, she followed Storm with the whip pointed at her hindquarters, just enough to get her to start walking. At the same time, she said "walk" in a clear, distinct voice. When the mare had circled the corral and was almost back where she had started, it looked as though she was ready to stop. Instead of keeping her going, Janet decided to add another command. "Ho," she said.

Storm stopped, and Janet approached to give her a pet and a carrot. "Good girl," she said. "Good Storm."

Janet tried these two commands for several more passes, always sure to tell Storm "ho" right before it looked as if she was ready to stop on her own. Each time, she fed Storm another carrot. It didn't take Storm long to realize that if she stopped when Janet said "ho," she'd get a nice treat.

This is going great, Janet thought. *Time for the real*

stuff. "Let's go for a trot. Trot!" she yelled. To make her point that a trot was faster than a walk, she flicked the whip harder at Storm's hooves.

On cue, Storm went faster around the corral.

"Ho!" Janet cried.

Storm stopped dead in her tracks.

"Trot!" Janet said.

This time, she hardly had to use the whip at all. Storm knew just what to do.

"Awesome," Janet said aloud. Storm had come really far for one training session.

Since it was going so well, Janet taught Storm "canter," and then she turned her around and lunged her in the opposite direction. More than anything, it was important to develop the horse's abilities equally on each side so that no matter what the judges asked for, Storm could do it.

J.G. came around as Janet was taking Storm off the line and letting her run around the corral without any commands. "How'd it go?" he asked.

"Like a dream," Janet said. "This is one smart horse. Once she has the voice commands down, I'll get the vocal signals going with my cues," Janet said, watching Storm frolic happily. "That may be a bit tougher."

J.G. smiled, looking straight into Janet's eyes. "A bit. Let me know if you need any help."

"I sure will," Janet said, trying not to blush. The more time she spent with J.G., the more she liked him. She just hoped it didn't show too much.

After a few more lessons on the lunge line, Janet was ready to saddle Storm and work on leg and rein cues. Later, she'd work on getting a smooth contact going so that whenever she gave Storm a command, her moves would be clean and effortless. For now, it was important to make sure Storm knew how to read the voice, leg, and rein signals all together.

Once again, Storm was a dream. She quickly learned that a light squeeze meant "walk," and that increasingly vigorous pressure from Janet's legs to her barrel meant "trot" and "canter." Before, Storm had needed hard kicks to get her going; after just a few lessons—and quite a few carrots—Storm could easily tell the difference between Janet's leg signals. The same was true for the rein cues. Janet didn't need to pull up on the bit to get Storm to halt. Just the slightest pressure of the reins between Janet's fingers got Storm to slow, then stop.

It was so easy to train Storm that Janet had to scratch her head each night as she let Storm loose to gallop around the corral. Sure, the horse had already been broken in, but she was quickly changing from a temperamental ranch horse into a green show horse. Janet knew horses well enough to know that eventually they napped or refused to do the moves. The question was, when would the trouble start with Storm?

She thought for sure it would be when she got into the saddle and tried to get Storm to ride on contact. According to her grandfather, this was where the real challenges came in. When you asked the horse to move in an organized way, sometimes other things fell apart. Since this would be the main thing the judges would be looking for when she rode eq, she knew it would be the toughest test of her ability as a trainer.

The afternoon came for Janet to mount Storm and work on her moves as a rider. She was nervous, but excited, too, and as she raced through her chores at the stables, she wondered what would happen. Would Storm still be her dream horse? Or would she balk and become difficult?

Down at the ranch, Storm was waiting in her stall, eager and ready for her lesson.

"Come on, girl," Janet said to her. "Today's the big day." She tacked Storm, led her to the corral, and mounted her. "Tell you what," she said. "We'll start on something simple."

Janet walked Storm slowly around the corral. She started out with loose reins. Gradually, she crept up on the reins until there was very little slack left in them. Next, she urged the mare on until the remaining slack was gone. Now the key was to let the reins and the bit follow the movement of the horse. This was the kind of subtlety the judges would be looking for.

Janet took several turns, careful to keep the proper contact with her hands. Her grandfather had taught her that the way to do this was to pretend that the reins were silk threads and that if they became slack, the horse would gallop over a cliff. Too tight, and the bit would cut the horse's mouth.

Once she was satisfied with her own form, she got ready to stop. "Halt," she said, softly pulling up on the reins.

Storm's head came up, and her mouth opened. Janet felt the vibration of the bit in her mouth.

"Too hard," she told herself. "Try again."

The next time, Storm did better. She came to a standstill with her head and neck at about the same position as when she was walking. And Janet's moves were smoother, too. She remembered this time to give a little with the reins just after Storm stopped.

"Looking good," a voice called from the porch. It was Larissa. She stepped off the porch and walked toward the corral. "How's it going?"

"Pretty well, I guess," Janet said. "You tell me."

She practiced going from a walk to a halt, with Larissa looking on and giving feedback. Between the two of them, they managed to get Storm's halt to the point where it was as smooth as any Janet had seen. It really helped to have someone else watching from the side, someone who could tell Janet if the moves worked.

"We make a pretty good team," Janet said, dismounting.

"I guess we do," Larissa said with a smile.

Janet fed Storm a carrot piece, then untacked her and allowed her to run the corral. "Storm's a good horse," she said. "Smart, a quick learner."

"You really think she can win, don't you?" Larissa said.

"I know she can." Judging from how fast Storm had learned so far, and how much time they had left, Janet was sure of it. "You'll see. She'll be winning loads of ribbons."

Larissa raised an eyebrow. "Maybe. If she doesn't take off on you and bolt. Remember, this is a horse that needs to roam."

Larissa walked away, skeptical. Janet turned back to Storm, disappointed. She knew Larissa still didn't believe it was possible to train Storm, but how could she ignore what she'd already taught Storm to do?

From then on, Janet noticed that Larissa came around a lot when she was training Storm. At first, Janet was sure she just wanted to keep an eye on her, to make sure she was treating Storm right. But after a while, she began to wonder if maybe Larissa wasn't just a little curious about what Storm was learning to do. If that was the case, she didn't mind at all, since she actually found it helpful to have Larissa watch and tell her how she and Storm looked. Working this way, Janet could train Storm in half the time. After a month or so, Storm had mastered nearly all the moves she'd need for the eq class.

All except backing up, that was. Every time Janet got on the mare and pulled back on the reins, Storm bucked and threw her. After getting dumped a dozen times, Janet decided to move on. Backing up would just have to wait. But she couldn't avoid it forever. A judge was going to ask them to do it—eventually.

"Maybe she thinks you're asking her to buck,"

Larissa said with a smile one afternoon when Storm had dumped Janet for the tenth time.

"Very funny," Janet said, dusting off her jeans and getting ready to remount. "Is that a trick you taught her?"

She remounted and walked Storm around the ring, then brought her to a halt. The move was smooth and effortless. Storm's head and shoulders remained in exactly the same position as when they'd been walking. Then she gently pulled straight back, keeping the reins even.

"Back!" she said, giving the command.

Instead of taking a step backward, Storm raised her front hooves. Janet hung on for dear life as the mare pawed the air with her legs.

"Rats!" Janet said, slipping off the rear and landing with a thud in the dirt.

Larissa laughed. "It looks like you've both had it. Maybe you'd better give up for the day."

"No way," Janet said, determined. "This horse is going to learn to be obedient if it's the last thing I do."

But it was no use. Storm just wouldn't learn.

"It's not going to do us any good to go into the arena with a horse that can't back up," Janet said, untacking the horse and giving up for the day. The days were getting shorter, and it was dark by five. Thanksgiving was almost here, which meant Christmas was not far behind. After that it would be January, and Janet hadn't even started training Storm for the jumps yet. Even though

Storm was smart, she'd taken longer to learn the eq moves than Janet thought she would. Correction, Janet thought. Teaching Storm how to back up had taken a lot longer than she thought it would.

"Maybe you need a break," Larissa said. "Take a week off. Give Storm a rest."

Janet thought about Larissa's advice as she groomed Storm. The older girl was probably right. She'd been training the mare hard, and she'd come really far. It seemed as if she'd been training her a long time, but it had only been six weeks or so. Sometimes a horse didn't even master vocal commands in that time. It was just that they were so close to being really trained. She hated the thought that there was one move—and a really important one—that Storm still couldn't do. But she also knew that Larissa had a point: maybe Storm was tired. Maybe she was tired, too.

She was still trying to figure out what to do when her mother announced at dinner that night that they'd all be going to San Jose for Thanksgiving to visit her grandparents. "Your father can't take Christmas off," her mother said. "So we're going now instead. Is that okay?"

"Is that okay?" Janet asked in disbelief. "When do we leave?" There was only one thing she'd like to do more than train Storm, and that was visit her grandparents. Besides, Janet thought, if anyone would have a trick or two to help with Storm, it was her grandfather.

Her mother smiled. "I know this hasn't been the easiest time for you, Janet. But your father and I are really proud of how well you're doing. You seem to have made the adjustment okay."

"I guess," Janet said. She didn't have the heart to tell her mother that Hallie wasn't speaking to her and that none of the girls at the stables said hello anymore.

But Janet's mother wasn't a mother for nothing. "What's Hallie been up to?" she asked, her voice casual. "You two don't seem to hang out together much anymore."

"I see her at the stables," Janet said. "The truth is, she's got a boyfriend." Janet rolled her eyes.

Her mother seemed surprised. "A boyfriend? Really?"

"Yep," she said.

"So no more time for her girlfriends, huh?" her mother guessed.

"Something like that." Janet finished loading the dishwasher, relieved that her mother seemed to believe her excuse for why Hallie wasn't coming around.

During the drive up to San Jose, Janet thought of the questions she would ask her grandfather: Was she going about training Storm right? Was there anything she could do about the fact that Storm wouldn't back up? And were there any other tricks he could show her to help?

She couldn't wait to tell him about Storm. So far, no one else knew, and Janet realized she was dying to talk to someone. If anyone would understand Janet's love for horses, it was her Grandfather Cam.

After being on the road for what felt like ages, they left the interstate and took the road toward Gilroy. The brown hills rolled by on either side, dotted with big cottonwoods. They drove past vegetable stands where you could buy home-grown garlic, olives, almonds, and apricots, and through the sleepy town of Gilroy itself. About three miles outside of town, they came to her grandparents' driveway—which was more like its own road, since the ranch was set at least two miles back. As the Volvo bumped over the rutted road, Janet felt her excitement rise another notch. On either side, she saw cattle and horses grazing in the fields. Up ahead, she spotted the comfortable, two-story ranch house, one she knew had been shipped in boxes from a Sears in the Midwest— when you could still order houses like that—and put together by her great-grandfather himself.

"Grandpa!" Janet shouted, even before the car had come to a stop. "Grandma!"

Janet's grandparents came running down the steps, huge smiles on their faces. "We've been expecting you for an hour," her grandmother said, pulling her toward her with a big bear hug.

"What took you so long?" her grandfather asked.

Janet's grandfather had snow-white hair, combed back from his tanned face. Even at the age of seventy, he was still spry and in good shape. He gave his son a hug, then swooped down on Janet, lifting her high into the air.

"Grandpa!" she squealed. "Put me down!"

"Cam Marshall, our girl's too old for that nonsense," her grandmother said. "Now cut it out." Janet's mother and grandmother hugged each other. "You folks hungry?" her grandmother asked. "I've got cold chicken and some potato salad."

"Are we hungry?" her mother asked. "These two wanted to stop at that place in Buellton for pea soup, but I made Bob keep going. I wasn't going to ruin my appetite with that food."

Janet's grandmother smiled. "Good. Well, let's not stand around here gawking at one another. Let's eat!"

CHAPTER EIGHT

ey, Janet," Cam Marshall whispered, leaning toward her so only she could hear. "Wanna see how the new foal is doing?"

It was several hours later. Janet and her parents and grandparents were sitting in the living room, eating brownies and gossiping. Janet didn't want to be rude. But the truth was, she couldn't wait to be alone with her grandfather, so she could tell him about Storm.

"You bet I do!" she said. "Let's go."

"Whew," he said, once they were outside. "You looked like you needed a break from all that talk about as much as I did. Come on, I'll show you the filly."

Last spring, Janet's favorite mare Damsel had given birth to a filly. Over the summer, the foal had still been nursing at her dam. But now she was big enough to eat hay and oats, and strong enough to trot around the corral without being guided by her mother. Janet watched the foal as her thin brown legs carried her around the arena. With the white blaze on her forehead and the white socks around her hooves, the foal was a treasure.

"She'll make a great show horse," her grandfather said. "Too bad you can't come up here to train her. I could teach you something about breaking in a horse."

Janet practically laughed out loud. Leave it to her grandfather to bring up the one thing that was on her mind. "Actually, I've been training a horse down in Pasadena."

"You have?" her grandfather said. "Your father didn't mention anything about that."

"It's kind of a surprise," Janet said. "I'm waiting until I show her to let my mom and dad see. There's a season opener at the end of February. I want to ride Storm— that's the horse—in it. I just know we can win ribbons, Grandpa. I know we can."

Her grandfather smiled, a broad white smile in the middle of his tanned, lined face. "You've got horses in your blood, Janet. Don't let anyone tell you otherwise."

It felt so good to be with her grandfather, talking about horses with someone else who cared. She just wished she could take him back home with her, to show him Storm and the ranch. Then everything would be perfect. Or almost perfect, if Storm weren't giving her such a hard time.

"The truth is," she said. "I'm having a little trouble with the horse."

"What kind of trouble?"

"You're not going to believe this," Janet said, shaking her head. "But she won't back up."

Her grandfather's laugh rang loudly across the corral. Even Damsel looked up. "You got you a horse that only goes forward, huh? What do you do, turn her around when you want to go the other way?" Even Janet had to smile. Put this way, Storm's problem really did sound funny. For some reason, she wasn't worried about it so much, especially when her grandfather put an arm around her shoulder and said, "Come on, I'll show you a trick. Maybe it will work on that horse of yours. The one without a reverse button."

Her grandfather went into the barn and came back to the arena with two halters, a lunge line, and a crop. First, he tethered the mare to a rail. Then he bridled the filly, who put up a little fuss when the bit went in.

"We've had her on a lead before," he said. "But this is the toughest part. This little girl just doesn't like the bit." Finally, he got the filly to accept the bit. "Okay," he said. "Let's pretend this here filly knows all her other moves, and we're ready to teach her backing up. Come here, kiddo. I can't do this without you."

Janet hopped over the rail and went to help her grandfather. "What can I do?"

"Stand next to the filly, just to the side of her," he instructed. "Now put the reins over her head as if you were riding her."

Janet did as her grandfather said. "Now what?"

"Now take the reins in your hand about eight inches

from the bit. Pull back—gently now—and use your voice command at the same time."

"Back," Janet said, pulling on the reins.

The filly didn't budge.

Cam Marshall smiled. "Looks like we got us a good subject, huh?" he said. "Is she about as stubborn as your mare?"

"Not quite," Janet said. "My mare doesn't just stand still. She bucks and throws me."

"Every time?" Janet's grandfather asked.

"Every time," Janet confirmed.

Her grandfather shook his head. "Janet, it's up to the rider to teach the horse obedience. You should know that by now."

"I know," Janet said. "But how?"

"With this." He held up the crop. "Ready?"

"Ready," Janet said.

She went through the same moves as before, calling "back" and pulling on the reins. This time, her grandfather snapped the crop at the filly's front legs, just above the hooves. Like magic, the filly stepped back.

"See?" he said with a smile. "No horse is going to stand still for the crop. She stepped back to avoid the punishment."

Janet calmed the filly.

"Let's try it again," her grandfather said. "This time, you use the crop."

Janet gave the command, pulling back on the reins with one hand and aiming the crop with the other. She didn't like striking the filly, but she knew her grandfather was right. The only way to teach a horse obedience was to use the crop. When the filly took two steps backward, her grandfather reached out to give the animal a treat.

"Good girl," he said. "Again."

After ten more tries, her grandfather told Janet to try it without the crop. "A lesson's no good unless she's learned the vocal," he said.

Janet pulled on the reins and called "back." This time, the filly actually stepped back without the crop. "Wow," Janet said. "It worked."

"Sure it did," her grandfather said. "Think it'll do for that ornery mare of yours?"

"Let's hope so," Janet said with a smile, feeling sure that it would.

Janet couldn't wait to get home and try out the move. The second their car hit the driveway, she grabbed her knapsack, took it upstairs, then headed back out. "I'm going down to the stables," she yelled to her parents. "See you soon."

"Janet!" Liz Marshall cried. "It's four o'clock on a Sunday afternoon. What could you possibly need to do down there?"

"I've got to feed Duke," Janet said, fumbling for an excuse. "I promised Hallie I would, since she's not coming home until tomorrow."

"Okay," Janet's mother said with a sigh. "But be back

here by six. It's been a long weekend, and you've got school tomorrow."

Janet raced down to the ranch and immediately went to the barn to saddle Storm. J.G. was there, tending to his own horse, Paint. "Janet!" he said, giving her a big hello. "How's it going?"

"Great," Janet said. There were those eyes again, she thought. They never ceased to amaze her. "I think I have a trick for getting Storm to back up."

"Do you?" he asked. "Well, let's see."

J.G. reached for Storm's halter just as Janet went to get the horse. Their hands touched momentarily, and Janet's stomach did an upside-down flop.

"Sorry," J.G. said.

"No problem," Janet told him. "My fault."

Her stomach was still in knots when she led Storm into the corral. Larissa came out from the ranch house to watch.

"So what's the trick?" J.G. asked.

Janet took a crop in one hand and trailed the reins over Storm's neck with the other. With the crop at Storm's front hooves, she pulled back on the reins. Naturally, the mare reared.

"Watch this," she said.

As she got ready to swat the mare with the crop, she held her breath. Her grandfather had made it seem so easy. But Storm wasn't some impressionable filly. Would Storm take the cue, or would she still balk?

"Here goes nothing," she said.

This time, when she pulled back on the reins, Janet snapped the crop at the mare's front hooves. Suddenly, Storm wasn't rearing back anymore. Her front hooves came down on the ground and she took a quick step backward.

Storm seemed surprised at the move. Even Janet was amazed. Just to be sure, she tried it again. Again, Storm danced backward to get away from the crop.

"It worked!" Janet cried. "All right!"

"Wow!" Larissa's eyes were wide with surprise. She hugged her brother, who came over to hug Janet.

"You did it," J.G. said, pulling her close. "Nice job!"

Janet froze in J.G.'s arms. She hadn't ever been hugged by a boy before. Of course, it didn't really mean a thing. Except that it felt pretty nice.

"I guess you were right," J.G. said, standing back and giving Janet an appreciative look. "Maybe Lady really can be a show horse."

"There's no maybe about it," Janet said, still reeling—though she wasn't sure whether it was from Storm finally being able to back up or from J.G.'s hug. They both felt pretty good. "We're going to win a ribbon. Just you wait and see."

Training Storm was a treat. Training Sugar was another thing entirely. The gelding was giving Janet so much trouble that she had pretty much given up. And Sugar knew it. When Janet was passing his stall at the stables the next day, the horse looked up at her from under his sad brown eyes and gave a small nicker.

"You're right, you're right," Janet said apologetically. "I have been neglecting you. All that ends today—I promise."

Before Thanksgiving, Connie had taken Janet aside and asked her why she hadn't been training Sugar. Every day since then that Janet didn't take the gelding out into the ring, Janet felt Connie's disapproving look. If Janet really did want to compete in the opener, the look seemed to say, she sure wasn't acting like it. There was no getting around it. She'd have to ease up on training Storm and get down to some serious work on Sugar.

Janet led Sugar to the grooming area, hooked him up by his lead, and got out her tack box. First, she took a curry comb to Sugar's hide, working the dirt out from under his legs and belly. Next, using a set of electric clippers, Janet trimmed Sugar's whiskers, along with the hair around his eyes, ears, fetlocks, and coronet areas. Afterward, she checked Sugar's hoofs, picked out the dirt, and put some dressing on them.

Since Sugar hadn't had a bath in a while, Janet wet him down and lathered him with warm, soapy water. Then she used a sweat scraper on his sides to get him dry quickly. Even in the warm California climate, a wet horse could end up a sick horse. After properly grooming Sugar, Janet stood back to admire her work.

"Looking good," a voice said as Janet finished wiping down Sugar's coat. Janet turned to see Connie. "Are you prettying him up for a reason, or did you just want to see him pretty?"

Janet felt another pang. It was one thing to know she'd been neglecting the horse. But it was another thing to have Connie point it out to her. She picked up her equipment and put it all back inside her tack box. "I realize I haven't been completely on top of things—"

"Janet, it's up to you," Connie interrupted her. "If you want to win a ribbon, then you have to ride."

"I know that," Janet grumbled.

"So let's ride," Connie said. "I haven't given you a jumping lesson in a while, have I?"

Janet shook her head.

"Well, let's do it," Connie said enthusiastically. "You and I both know you're just as good a rider as anyone else your age. But if you don't apply yourself..."

Connie's voice trailed off as she disappeared inside the tack room to get Sugar's saddle. Janet wanted to tell Connie just how much she'd been applying herself—on another horse. Connie returned with a saddle and bridle. Janet quickly tacked and mounted Sugar and led him to the ring for their lesson.

"Okay, kiddo," Connie said. "Let's see your stuff."

The practice ring was laid out with single jumps on the outside, then an in-and-out on the inside. The in-and-out meant that Janet would have one stride after the first jump to get the horse ready for the second jump. She decided to take the outside jumps first and work on her approach.

Janet made sure to point her horse straight at the middle of the jump. Then she drove her heels down hard, gripped with her legs, and leaned forward. A second later, she and Sugar were flying over the jump, with a nice landing on the other side.

"Good work," Connie said. "Watch your follow-through."

Janet headed around the ring and got ready to take the next jump. This time, she bounced a bit on the landing and found herself on the wrong lead.

"Change lead," Connie yelled. "Get on the right lead."

Janet gave the rein and leg cue to Sugar to get back on the inside lead so that he was cantering with his right foot forward. After a slightly awkward transition, in which the horse stumbled and Janet bounced, she was on the right lead.

"Nice!" Connie said. "Way to go. Watch out for your transition."

Janet took a few more of the outside jumps, then got ready for the in-and-out on the inside. She circled Sugar around, pulled him in, then squeezed. As they approached the first jump, Janet concentrated hard. She must have been concentrating too hard, though, because just as he came to the jump, Sugar refused.

Janet landed on Sugar's neck as the horse stopped short. "Sugar!" she hissed. "Don't make me look bad."

She wheeled him around and went back to try the jump again.

Again, Sugar refused.

"Darn horse," Janet said under her breath. She really wanted to get the in-and-out with Connie watching.

"Don't let him lead you," Connie said. "You've got to make him take the jump."

"I'm trying," Janet said.

"Keep your eyes forward," Connie said. "Don't drop your weight."

This time, she kept her eyes up and looked at a point on the far side of the jump. This had to help Sugar keep his balance!

Not a chance. The second he got to the jump, Sugar refused.

"Try again."

She did. But each time, Sugar stopped just short of the fence. "I don't know what I'm doing wrong," Janet said in despair. "He took the outside jumps. Maybe he doesn't like the in-and-out."

"No way," Connie said. "He doesn't even know there's another jump after this one. Keep going."

"Okay," Janet said, trying not to sound exasperated.

Over and over, she attempted to get the horse to take the jump. Over and over, Sugar refused. Finally, even Connie must have seen that it was no use. The horse just wasn't going to take the jump that day.

"All right, Janet," she said. "Let's call it a day. We'll try again tomorrow."

Janet felt her insides twist with frustration. Storm wouldn't have given her such a hard time. So much for taking care of Sugar. As far as she was concerned, even with all that attention and a full grooming, the horse was still too lame to ride.

As Janet was leading Sugar out of the ring, Hallie was coming in. "Hi," she said. "Too bad about the jumps."

"Yeah," Janet said. "I guess he's having a lousy day."

"Maybe," Hallie said. "Maybe not. I heard from Aloe that Sugar's been spooked ever since he took that fall a few weeks ago. He hasn't done an in-and-out since."

"Is that right?" Janet asked.

Hallie raised an eyebrow. "I guess. Hope you're not counting on Yankee. You heard that Becky leased him?"

"She did?" It was news to Janet, but then again she hadn't really been listening to the barn gossip. Not that she had her hopes set on Yankee anymore. She just hated the idea of Becky getting yet another horse. "Since when?"

"You really haven't been paying attention, Marshall, have you?" Hallie asked. "Two weeks ago, MacDougal got sick. Becky's mom said that she didn't want her to lose any time training, so she agreed to let her lease Yankee."

"No kidding. That's great." *Terrific,* Janet thought. Her smile felt frozen on her face.

"Yep." Hallie chucked Duke to get him moving. "So I guess you really are stuck with Sugar."

"I guess so," Janet said.

Janet left the ring, dismounted, and went to untack Sugar. Outside, the sun was setting and the sky had grown dark. As she led Sugar back to his stall to curry him and feed him his oats, Janet tried not to think about the what-ifs: what if Storm couldn't get all the moves? What if Sugar never did learn to take the in-and-out? What if Becky beat her on Yankee? What if she and Hallie never spoke to each other again?

She took a last look at Sugar, then decided to hurry through the rest of her chores. Right now, the stables didn't feel like a very friendly place. She did her usual mucking and grooming in about half the time. Then she grabbed her jacket and headed home without even saying good-bye to Connie.

An hour later, the Marshalls were sitting down to eat when the phone rang. It was Connie, looking for Janet.

"What is it?" Janet asked her mother as she handed her the phone. Connie had never called her at home before.

"I don't know," Mrs. Marshall said. "It sounds important."

Janet took the receiver from her mother and said hello. "What's up?" she asked. "Is something wrong?"

Connie's voice was tense. "I'm not sure," she said. "We still don't know. Janet, I have to ask you something important. You put Sugar away this afternoon, right?"

"Sure I did," Janet said. "After I untacked him. Why?"

"Did you close his stall door and lock it?" Connie asked.

"I think so. Why?"

"Janet, Sugar's gone."

"Gone?" Janet said. "What do you mean gone?"

"His stall is empty, and he's nowhere to be found." Connie sighed. "Janet, you know there's only one way this could have happened. And that's if you forgot to close the stall and shut him in. As far as I'm concerned, you were responsible for this horse. And that means you're responsible for him being missing, too."

CHAPTER NINE

*J*anet couldn't believe what she was hearing. Sugar was gone, and Connie was blaming her.

"But I'm sure I closed the stall door," Janet said. "I mean, I'm almost positive."

"'Almost positive' isn't good enough, Janet. Everyone knows Sugar likes to bolt. The door needs to be locked. We have no idea how long he's been gone, but we're organizing a search party." Connie paused. "I think it would be a good idea for you to come back and help look for him. Bring a flashlight and some warm clothes. Tell your parents we'll be out late, but I'll make sure you get home by eleven."

"Sure," Janet said. "I'll be right over."

She hung up the phone and tried to think past the knot in her stomach. She'd locked the stall door. Or had she? She tried to retrace her steps, but it was useless. She'd been upset when she left the stables, and there was a good chance she'd forgotten to lock the door. It really *was* her fault that Sugar was missing.

"I have to go back to the stables," she told her parents. "Sugar's missing, and they need me to help look for him." She left out the part about Connie blaming her. She really didn't want her parents to yell at her, not with Connie already so mad. "I have to go, but Connie said I should be home by eleven."

The Marshalls looked at Janet with concern. "Do what you have to do, sweetie. We'll be here if you need us."

The whole way back to the stables, Janet went over and over her last moves, the way she might if she had lost something and needed desperately to find it. She'd taken Sugar back, untacked him, then taken the saddle and bridle to the tack room. Had she tied him up before or after? She couldn't remember. And had she closed the stall door behind her as she left the horse? She just couldn't remember!

By the time she got to the stables, Janet was nearly in tears. If only she could go back and redo those last few minutes. She'd been upset and worried and distracted. She knew that wasn't the right mood to be in when caring for a horse. But she couldn't take it back, not now. Right now, she had to do whatever she could to help find Sugar.

At the stables, all the lights were on. Janet could see Connie talking to a group of people by the stable offices.

She got there just as Connie was giving them all instructions about looking for Sugar.

"I'm dividing you up into teams of two," Connie said. "We're going to cover this area from top to bottom, from the stables down into the arroyo and up to the street. We'll go as far south as Huntington Drive and as far north as Devil's Gate. There are twenty of us. We'll all meet back here at eleven. I don't want you kids out any later than that. If you find Sugar, do your best to bring him back down. If he won't come, then head back here for help. Above all, don't do anything dangerous or rash. The point is not to cause any more trouble. Okay?

"Here are the teams." Connie went down a list of pairs and where she was sending each team. When Janet heard her name, she was amazed to find herself paired with Hallie. Hallie raised her hand to object, but Connie didn't want to hear about it. "You two used to be able to work together. It's time for you to solve your problems and try it again. I've given you the lower arroyo. Stick to this side of the creek. I seriously doubt Sugar's crossed it, and besides it's not safe on the other side. If we have to look there later, I'll put together a bigger group and we can search in the daylight. All right, people. Let's move!"

While Aloe, Becky, and all the others found their partners and headed off to search, Janet and Hallie hesitated. Pretty soon, they were the only two standing there.

"Well," Janet said, looking anywhere but at Hallie.

"Huh," said Hallie, gazing past Janet.

"Looks like we got stuck with one another, huh?" Janet said.

"Looks like," Hallie agreed.

Fine, Janet thought. Since Hallie didn't feel like talking, she didn't either. She flicked on her flashlight and led the way out of the stables toward a trail that led to the arroyo. It probably wouldn't help to look for hoofprints or droppings. Some of the more daring horse owners up and down this side of the arroyo were known to take their animals on trails that wound through here. Sure enough, as they took the trail that wound past the stable area and down into the arroyo, she saw a lot of hoofprints. When they got to the gate that led into the arroyo itself, it was standing wide open.

"He'd have no problem getting through," Janet said, half to herself, half out loud. "You know, something bothers me about this idea. I doubt Sugar even likes the arroyo. I get the feeling he'd be afraid."

"Connie said that he once belonged to an owner who took him down here," Hallie told her. "He wouldn't be afraid—he'd be used to it. Besides, you know how he likes to wander."

Hallie's comment felt like criticism. If she'd remembered that Sugar liked to wander, Hallie seemed to be saying, she'd have seen to it that Sugar was locked in. Janet bristled. Of course they all knew that Sugar had been known to turn up in the parking lot of the supermarket down the street from the stables, and the golf course two miles away. Most horses never strayed far from home, but Sugar was different. Connie said that it was his mustang blood, though Janet thought it was probably just a bad sense of direction. In this case, Sugar's bad sense of direction might even have led him down into the arroyo. It sure didn't help to have Hallie remind her of her mistake.

Owls hooted to one another and the wind rustled through the ash trees. In the brush, Janet heard night animals scrounging for food. She knew that anything big would sound loud in the leaves. Once, she'd been camping with her parents and heard a huge noise in the woods, like a bear. She had called out, "Hey, bear, hey, bear!" to scare the animal away, only to hear her father's laughter in reply. He'd gone into the woods to use the bathroom. Janet then had known firsthand that the sound of a person walking on leaves was not that much different from the sound of a bear.

Or a horse, for that matter, Janet thought, keeping her ears open for something louder than just the small rustling noises of mice and birds. "Sugar!" she called out. "Here, Sugar!"

As they walked along the trail, Hallie joined her in calling out for the horse. Within an hour, Janet and Hallie had covered the near side of the arroyo all the way up to Devil's Gate. There, the trail came to a stop at the mountains. For Sugar to get any farther, he would have to climb the steep mountain trail that ran next to the creek. Above, Janet could hear the roar of a waterfall as the creek came out the mountain gorge.

"Well, that takes care of that," Hallie said, the exasperation clear in her voice. "I knew that stupid horse didn't come down here."

"We don't know that," Janet said. "He might have."

"But he didn't," Hallie said. "He's not here, Marshall. We looked up and down this whole arroyo."

"Only on this side," Janet said, scanning the dark brush across the creek. "He might have crossed over."

"Yeah, right," said Hallie. "And I'm a monkey's uncle. That horse is terrified of water. No way he'd cross that creek. And even if he tried to, he'd never make it across."

"We have to look," Janet said, heading toward the creek. She knew that on the other side, it ran close by the Gradys' ranch, but having Hallie find the ranch—or even think of it again—was just a risk she'd have to take. "I'm going over."

"No way, Marshall," Hallie said, grabbing on to Janet's arm. "I'm not letting you."

"Why not?" Janet asked, surprised. "I wouldn't think you cared."

"It's not safe, for one," Hallie said, ignoring Janet's comment. "And because there's no way Sugar could be over there. Besides, it's ten-fifteen. We have to go back to the stables."

Hallie turned to head back down the trail. Janet watched her go and wondered if now was the time to try making up, for real. She felt as if Hallie was ready to be

112

friends again, but somehow she just still couldn't manage it.

As she walked along behind Hallie, she glanced at the creek and the woods on the other side every now and then. Somehow, she had a feeling it was worth looking there. But Hallie was right—they were supposed to meet back at the stables in forty-five minutes. Right now, there wasn't enough time.

Connie and the others were already there by the time Janet and Hallie came trudging up from the arroyo. From the expression on Connie's face, Janet could tell that no one had been able to find Sugar.

"Okay, everyone, listen up," Connie said, gathering the group around her by the stable office. "It's late. I want you all to go home. Tomorrow morning, I'll see if we can't send some more search parties. Those of you who have school, maybe you can come by and look for him afterward. I know we'll find that horse," she said with determination. "He's probably lost and can't find his way home. One way or another, he'll turn up. Don't worry."

Aloe, Becky, Cody, and the other girls seemed to brighten at Connie's pep talk. But it wasn't enough for Janet. So far, no one had said anything to her personally. Still, she could feel it in the looks she got. She hadn't tied him up, or she hadn't closed his stall. Either way, she was responsible. If it weren't for her, Sugar would be happily dozing away in his stall instead of wandering around somewhere, lost and frightened.

Hallie's mother was waiting for her in the parking lot. Just before she left, Hallie seemed to hang back a bit. "See ya," Janet said. "Thanks for being my partner."

"No problem," Hallie said. "Too bad we didn't find him, huh?"

"Yeah," Janet agreed. "That would have been pretty incredible if we'd come out of the arroyo leading Sugar by the nose."

"Excitement," Hallie agreed. "Well, see you around."

"Sure," Janet said.

It didn't count as making up, but Janet felt a little better. That was, until Connie motioned for her to follow her into her office.

"Well, Janet," Connie began as she sat down behind her desk. "You already know that I hold you responsible for this fiasco."

"I know," she said. "And I'm ready to take the blame, believe me I am." There was no point in denying it: Sugar was her responsibility. "I'm really, really sorry. I promise you it won't ever happen again, not in a million years."

"No, it won't," Connie agreed. "You're right."

A wave of relief passed over her. So Connie trusted her after all! "I don't know what happened, but I'm glad you can see how it was all a mistake. I never meant—"

Connie gazed at her intently. "I didn't say that, Janet," she said. "I agree it was a mistake, but I was serious when I said it wouldn't happen again."

"Why not?" A sinking feeling replaced the relief

she'd had just a second ago. "I'm not sure what you mean."

"I'm going to have to let you go," Connie said.

"What?" Janet couldn't believe her ears. "You're kidding, right?"

Connie shook her head sadly. "Sorry, but I'm not. As of tonight, you no longer have a job at San Pascual."

CHAPTER TEN

ou're firing me?" Janet was in shock. "I mean, I know I've made a mistake, a huge mistake. But you can't fire me, Connie. Please!"

"I can't keep you on here, Janet, not after this." Connie got up from her desk and began turning off the lights in the office, getting ready to go. "Not locking Sugar up isn't the only mistake you've made recently. I've already had complaints from some owners about your getting the feed wrong for their horses. And your grooming and mucking haven't been terrific either. I wasn't going to say anything, but now…"

"But you can't let me go!" Janet had to make Connie understand. She just had to. "I need to work here. I can't afford lessons otherwise, and then there's my training for the opener."

"On what?" Connie asked. "Sugar's missing, in case

you've forgotten. No, Janet. You haven't proved to me that I can trust you."

Before Janet could stop them, the tears were welling in her eyes. "Don't do this, Connie. Please. I said I was sorry. I promise I'll be more careful from now on. I'll keep better track of the feed, and I'll double my time on grooming. I promise!"

Connie's gaze softened a bit. Janet tried not to let her hopes get too high. Would she change her mind? When she first met Connie, she knew they had something in common: they both loved horses so much that they'd do anything to ride. Would Connie remember that now?

Connie dropped her gaze and let out a long sigh. "It's been a long day," she said. "Let me think about all this overnight. There's no point in making a decision now. Go home, Janet. We'll talk tomorrow."

By now, the office was dark. Connie turned off the last light on her desk and made for the door. Janet wiped the tears from her eyes. There was no point in begging any more than she already had. She could kick herself for what had happened with Sugar. But she also knew that she had to accept the consequences. There was no getting around it.

Back home, her parents were waiting for her in the living room. "What happened?" her mother asked. "It's bad news, isn't it? You didn't find the horse?"

How could she tell her parents that the truth was

even worse than they suspected? She felt the tears come to her eyes again.

"Janet? What's wrong?" her father asked.

"Connie's going to fire me. Because I forgot to lock up Sugar and that's why he got loose. I said I was sorry," she said, crying between the words, "but she said it wasn't the only mistake I'd made, and that she wasn't sure she could still trust me. It was such a stupid thing to do! How could I have been so dumb?"

"Don't be so hard on yourself," her mother said. "It's just a job. We've all lost jobs before."

"Speak for yourself," her father said.

Leave it to her dad to make her laugh. "I guess you were never fired, huh, Dad?" she said, her nose thoroughly stuffed up by now.

"Not on your life," he said proudly. "I've always quit first."

"She said she might reconsider," Janet said.

"See?" her father said. "So there is a glimmer of hope after all."

"I guess." Janet was glad that her parents were taking her side, but she knew that Connie had a point, too. "Except that the truth is, Connie's right. I have been making mistakes, and not only with Sugar."

"I'm surprised," her mother said. "That's not like you."

"Is there some reason?" her father asked. "Something we should know about?"

Janet paused. The right thing to do would be to tell

118

her mom and dad about Storm. Wasn't that really why she'd been making mistakes at the stables? Because her mind was on the mare, and not on Sugar or the other animals? Because she rushed through her chores at San Pascual so that she could spend every free moment down at the ranch? The problem was, she still couldn't tell her parents about Storm. But it occurred to her that they might be able to help with her other problem: Hallie. If anyone understood Janet's stubborn streak and what to do about it, it was her mother.

"Actually, Hallie's not talking to me," Janet explained. "At least, she wasn't. And the other girls at the stables weren't either. Tonight, Hallie told me that Becky's leased Yankee, and I guess I was more upset about it than I thought. I kind of left in a hurry."

"So you didn't do your job right because you were thinking about what Hallie had told you," her mother said. "You must have been really upset. Why hadn't you told us what was going on with Hallie and the other girls?"

"I don't know," Janet said. "I guess I wanted to deal with it myself."

"But we're always here for you, Scooter," her father said. "You know that."

Even though it was nice to have them sympathize with her about Hallie, Janet felt ten times worse with her parents taking her side like this. She knew she still wasn't telling them the truth.

"But Connie's right, Mom," she said. "It *was* my fault about Sugar."

"It's true that Connie can't have you around if you're thinking more about your friends and what they're saying than you are about the horses," her mother agreed. "Especially when you've been hired to take care of them. But it's also true that it's not fair for Hallie and the other girls to treat you that way."

"Maybe Hallie's not so mad anymore," Janet said. "At least, she said good-bye to me tonight. That's a big step—for her, I mean."

"I guess that means it's up to you to make a step in her direction, huh?" her mother said.

"I guess."

"You don't sound very excited about the idea," her father said.

Of course she wasn't. "You know I hate to apologize," Janet said. "Besides, I got along without friends before Hallie, right?"

"And you were miserable," her mother pointed out. "Why is it so hard for you, Janet?" she asked. "Why can't you just say you're sorry and that you want to be friends again?"

Janet didn't have an answer. It was so easy to get along with J.G. and Larissa. And she thought about Storm and how easy it was to train her. Why couldn't things on this side of the creek be like that? Instead, there was always something to worry about, like Hallie or Sugar or Connie firing her or how not to lie to her parents without telling them everything. Instead of working

120

it all out, she just wanted to spend all her time at the ranch, with J.G. and Larissa and Storm. That would be easy.

"I don't know, Mom," she said wearily. "I wish I had an answer. I really do."

When Janet woke up the next morning, it was barely six. The kitchen was cold and dark. Even the coffee pot hadn't flicked on yet. She still had an hour and a half before she'd even have to think about getting ready for school. Over her bowl of cereal, it came to her: she knew where to find Sugar.

She drank a quick glass of juice, grabbed a banana, and headed outside. There was dew on the grass and a heavy mist in the air. She drew her jacket tight around her and headed for the arroyo.

The night before, she'd had this strange—and strong—feeling that Sugar had crossed the creek, but Hallie hadn't thought there was much point in looking. But now Janet knew that was exactly where she should look. If she could bring back Sugar, then everything would be fine. She wouldn't lose her job, Connie would forgive her. Maybe even Hallie would want to be her friend again.

After crossing the creek, Janet headed away from the ranch, taking the left fork of the trail instead of the right. Soon the path came to a dead end against the canyon wall. No sign of Sugar here. She headed back along the path, keeping her eyes and ears open. But by the time she'd gotten halfway to the ranch, she still hadn't spotted any fresh horse prints.

It had been at least two days since she'd seen the Gradys. Standing at the overgrown patch of sage and creosote where the path to the ranch started, that same warm feeling came over her. All around, the air seemed almost alive. The birds were louder, the sound of the wind more intense. She parted the branches and headed down the path, drawn instinctively to the ranch. The closer she came to the corral, the stronger the feeling got. The air grew warmer. The light took on an orange glow, bathing the clearing and the corral and the barn in a soft warmth.

Janet thought she knew why the ranch made her feel this way. It was her secret, a place only she knew about. If Connie and the others decided to look for Sugar here, she'd die. Maybe if she spent enough time at the ranch, all her other problems would slowly disappear. Or maybe she just wouldn't care about them so much.

She'd never come around so early, but Janet knew that ranch people rarely slept late. Sure enough, J.G. and Larissa were already up when she walked onto the front porch. The kitchen table had been cleared of breakfast. J.G. spotted Janet through the kitchen window and came to the door, a surprised look on his face.

"What's up?" he said, tucking in his shirt. "Something wrong?"

With his rumpled shirt and his sleepy expression,

J.G. was cuter than ever. Janet resisted the urge to tease him about the tuft of hair that was sticking up over his ear.

"There's a horse that's missing from the stables," she said instead. "It was my horse—well, a school horse, really, but I was in charge of him. I didn't lock him up properly and he got loose from his stall, and now he's missing. And what's even worse is that I might lose my job because of my mistake."

"Gosh, Janet," J.G. said. "I'm really sorry. Do you want help looking for him?"

"Maybe later," she said. "Right now, I've got to get back home before my parents wonder where I've been. I just thought I'd stop by and ask if you'd seen him. You haven't, have you?"

"No," said J.G. "But I'll keep my eyes open. What does he look like?"

"He's about fourteen years old—I'd say sixteen hands high," Janet said. "Brown with a white blaze on his forehead—"

Larissa came out of the house. "Who's brown with a white blaze on his forehead?" she asked.

"Janet's horse from the stables," J.G. said. "The guy went missing last night."

Even though she was dressed in her jeans and work shirt, Larissa still looked incredibly elegant. How did she do it? Janet wondered, looking down at her own flannel shirt and overalls, which on her said "slob." Would she ever have Larissa's style?

A concerned look appeared in Larissa's intense blue eyes. "Maybe we should go out looking now," she said, "before we get started with the other chores. I'll saddle up Lady."

Larissa headed off to the stables. J.G. reached out to rub Janet's shoulder with a reassuring hand. The touch sent a shiver down her spine. *Just the cold, Marshall,* she told herself, knowing it wasn't true.

"I'm sure he'll turn up," he said. "Larissa and I know every inch of this land. If he's here on our spread, we'll find him, no matter if he's stuck or sick or—"

A desperate cry from the barn cut him off. "J.G., Janet!" Larissa screamed. "Come here! Quick!"

Janet and J.G. looked at each another in confusion. Then J.G. raced for the barn, with Janet close behind. Inside, Janet spotted Larissa in Storm's stall. She was wringing her hands, and there were tears streaming down her face.

"It's Lady," she said. "Look!"

Janet and J.G. pushed their way into the stall. There, lying on her fresh hay, was Storm. Her stomach was swollen, and her breath was coming in fits and starts. Her beautiful black eyes were rolling back in her head, and every once in a while she let out a low moan.

"What is it?" Janet asked. "What's wrong?"

"Colic," J.G. said.

"Colic!"

Janet was stunned. She'd heard about the miserable

disease, but she'd never seen a horse experience it first-hand. Her heart broke for the horse, who looked up at her with a mournful expression.

"We've got to get her walking," J.G. said. "Come on—help."

For the next twenty minutes, Janet helped J.G. and Larissa walk the mare slowly around the paddock. Storm had no desire to take part in the exercise, but they dragged her in slow steps anyway. Janet checked her watch every five minutes, frantic about the horse but knowing that she couldn't stay forever. Finally, she knew she had to get home or else risk getting into even deeper trouble—this time with her parents.

"Maybe I should call a vet to come down here," she said. "Isn't colic dangerous if it's not treated?"

"Can be," J.G. agreed. "But I think we can take care of it ourselves. Living down here, we know quite a few home remedies. I guess the real question is, how did this horse get sick? What's she been eating?"

"Same feed as ever," Larissa said. She petted the mare's forehead and spoke to her softly to keep her calm. "Janet, did you notice her eating anything strange?"

At first, Janet was going to say no. But then she remembered how she'd ridden Storm two days before, and she felt her stomach drop. She'd had Storm out in the fields for a good run. They'd trained hard that day. She'd decided Storm had earned the right to gallop over the open country. She had untacked the horse and let her roam a bit. In that time, there was a good chance that Storm had eaten the wrong thing.

Looking at the horse now, and seeing her swollen belly heave, Janet felt worse than ever. Larissa had warned her about not letting Storm graze out in the fields. But she hadn't listened. Storm could have died, and it would have been all her fault.

"I had her out in the fields," she admitted. "Storm might have eaten some ragweed or something. I'm sorry."

Larissa drew in a sharp breath. "You know you're supposed to watch her at all times," she said. "You can't let her just wander and eat whatever she wants."

"I know," Janet said, her heart heavy. "I guess I just wasn't paying attention."

"It happens, Lar," J.G. said. "I've had two horses of my own get colicky on me. Sometimes they just wander off and you can't stop 'em from eating everything in sight."

Janet wanted to hug J.G. for defending her. But in the end, it was Larissa's opinion that mattered—Storm was her horse, and Janet was supposed to look after her while they were out riding. For a long moment, Larissa was quiet. Would Larissa tell Janet that she couldn't ever ride the horse again? Wasn't that what Janet would have done, if she were in Larissa's shoes? But when Larissa spoke again, her voice was calm and quiet. "There's nothing we can do except let Lady recover. We certainly won't be having any practice sessions for a while."

"How long will it take for her to get better?" Janet asked.

"She'll be feeling fine in a day or two," J.G. said. "But I think we should take it easy for a week at the least. We have to keep her on simple feed and let her walk out the gas."

A week? No training for a week? Looking at Storm's miserable expression, Janet didn't have the heart to get upset. It was her fault—all of it. Sugar was missing, and Storm was sick. She had no horses at all to ride now, but she couldn't feel sorry for herself either. She had no one to blame but herself.

CHAPTER ELEVEN

*J*anet held her breath and waited. Connie stared at her across her desk. "I'm ready for the bad news," Janet said finally. "Whatever you've decided, I can take it. Really."

Connie placed her hands on the desk in front of her and gazed at Janet with her serious brown eyes. "Janet, I still think that what you did was utterly irresponsible. And I'm still very disappointed in your performance lately."

At this point, Janet pretty much stopped listening. From what Connie had said so far, it could only mean bad news.

"But I've had some time to cool down and I've decided I'm going to let you keep your job," she finished.

Janet could hardly believe her ears. "You mean you're not going to fire me after all?"

"I'm putting you on probation," Connie said.

"Oh, Connie, you won't regret this, I promise—"

"I'm sure I won't," Connie said, cutting her off. "It seems only fair to put you on notice. Consider this your warning, Janet. If you make one more mistake, you're out."

There was no getting around the tone in Connie's voice. She meant what she said. From now on, Janet had better be perfect—not one more mistake.

"Connie, I promise you," she said. "I'm going to work harder than you've ever seen me work."

"I should hope so," Connie said. She had her schedule book in front of her now, the one in which she kept track of who rode what mounts and on what day. "As for a mount for the season opener," she continued. "I can't help you there. Every other school horse is booked. Unless you can persuade an owner to let you ride one of their horses, I'm going to have to scratch you from the event."

Scratch her!

"No!" Janet yelled, almost leaping from her seat. "You can't do that, please—"

Connie looked at her in confusion. "I don't get it, Janet. With Sugar gone and no other horses to ride, how do you plan to compete?"

On Storm, Janet wanted to say. If Connie scratched her, she couldn't show up the day of the event riding another horse. She had to keep her name registered, she just had to. But how could she convince Connie?

"What if Sugar shows up?" Janet said. "Please don't

scratch me until we know for sure that he's gone. He could come back anytime. You never know."

Connie sighed. "Okay, Janet," she said, obviously holding out little hope. They both knew that horses had great homing instincts, but the fact that Sugar still hadn't made it back was a bad sign. "Technically, we don't have to scratch you until the first day of the opener. I guess I can give you until then."

Janet wanted to jump for joy. Her job was saved, and so was her place in the opener. "Thank you so much, Connie," she said. "This means a lot to me, that you're giving me another chance. I won't let you down."

"We both know what will happen if you do," Connie said, smiling for the first time since Janet had walked into her office. "Just remember, Janet, if Sugar doesn't turn up eventually, I'm going to have to put your hours toward the cost of the horse. No more lessons in the near future."

"I understand," Janet said. "You're absolutely right."

When Janet left Connie's office, she felt better than she had in days. Out in the main ring, Hallie was training Duke. She stopped to watch Hallie put Duke through the course. *She looks good,* Janet thought. Hallie was taking three-foot six-inch jumps without a hitch. And her form was awesome—terrific follow-through, smooth transitions. Hallie would be incredibly surprised when Janet showed up on Storm for the season opener, but Janet could see that she would also give her some solid competition. Beating her wasn't going to be easy!

As Janet watched her friend concentrate intensely, she thought again about her mother's advice. Was it really so bad what Hallie had done? Hadn't she been known to tell a secret herself more than once, by accident?

Hallie dismounted and led Duke to the gate. She spotted Janet at the rail and gave her a small wave.

"You look great," Janet told her. "So does Duke."

"Thanks," Hallie said, patting her horse. "He's a good guy. So, I was wondering, what are you going to do, now that you can't ride Sugar in the event? Can Connie find you another horse to train?"

Janet could tell that Hallie wasn't asking to make her feel bad. She really seemed to care. "Not a chance," she said. "I'm lucky I still have a job."

"She didn't fire you?" Hallie asked.

"Nope," said Janet.

Janet was surprised when Hallie reached out to give her a high five and a smile and said, "Excitement! I'm glad. It would really stink if you couldn't hang out here." Hallie kicked at a thick clump of mud. "So, have you had any more dreams about that horse?" she asked. "The one you rode in the arroyo?"

"Not exactly," Janet said.

"Maybe we should try looking for it again," Hallie said. "You never know."

"I'm not sure." Janet didn't want Hallie to think she was being standoffish, so she said, "I'm not in the mood to get grounded again, you know?"

"Right." Hallie smiled. "I think I know what you mean."

"Well, see ya around," Janet said.

"See ya," Hallie echoed. She was about to lead Duke off to the barn when she turned around and said, "Listen, Aloe's having a party this weekend. Want me to see if she'll invite you?"

Janet had heard about the party, but she hadn't had any hope of getting invited. Hallie's offer was pretty nice, considering how most of the girls felt about her at this point. Briefly, Janet wondered if she'd have the nerve to ask J.G. to go with her. She smiled as she imagined the expressions on her friends' faces when she walked through the door with him.

"That would be great," Janet said. "I mean, if you don't mind asking her."

"No problem," Hallie said. "Well, I guess I'll see you tomorrow."

"See ya," Janet said.

As she finished her chores at the stables, Janet felt a lot better. It was nice to be making up with Hallie. By tomorrow, Storm would be ready to start training again. There might even be a party to look forward to that weekend. She almost forgot about Sugar until she passed his empty stall. Looking in at his feed bin, water bucket, and tie-up chain, Janet felt awful once again.

"I'll never, ever be so careless again in my life," she swore to herself. "I promise."

❧❧

On Monday, Storm was well enough for Janet to begin training her again. The mare was a bit rusty after being out of commission for a week, and the days were even shorter as Christmas approached, but Janet worked quickly to bring Storm up to speed. Soon she was fully trained in eq, and it was simply up to Janet to get her own moves controlled and precise. Jumping with Storm had never been a problem—the horse could handle everything up to a waist-high fence out in the fields. Janet set up a simple course in the corral, using old rails she had found in the barn and some sets of adjustable posts J.G. had made for her from scrap wood.

She worked the mare first on a series of outside jumps. Then she rearranged the rails and posts so that there was an in-and-out inside the corral. Storm had no problem keeping on the right lead through the jumps. And even though she sometimes landed on the wrong lead after the last jump, Janet quickly trained her to change back.

Janet was untacking Storm for the night when J.G. came around, looked at the darkening sky, and said, "Looks like a big storm's coming. Better not plan to train Storm for a few days."

Janet searched the sky for clouds. To her, the night seemed clear and bright. Even the weather report hadn't said anything about it.

But sure enough, Janet awoke that night to the sound of rain. The next morning, the streets were slick with water, and there didn't seem to be any letup in sight.

"Nice weather," her father said at breakfast that morning. "And I'm scheduled to drive to Orange County for an interview. Let's hope there aren't too many crazy drivers on the road."

Janet was staring out the window. All she could think of was the corral, full of mud, and Storm, pent up in her stall. So J.G. had been right after all. She was trying to decide if she should head down to the ranch anyway, when the phone rang.

"I wonder who that could be," her mother said, taking a sip of coffee. "It's still only seven-thirty."

Her mother went to answer the phone. "He's right here," she said a moment later, handing the phone to Janet's father.

Janet didn't think much of the phone call until she saw her father's face turn white. "Dad," she said. "What's wrong?"

Her father's hands shook as he replaced the receiver.

"What's happening?" she asked. "What's wrong?"

"It's Grandpa," her father said. "He had a heart attack last night. He's in the hospital."

Janet sank back in her chair. All the warmth seemed to go out of the kitchen. Now all she felt was how cold, wet, and rainy the day was. And all she could think about was her grandfather, lying in a hospital bed. "Grandpa had a heart attack?"

"Is he okay?" her mother asked. "When did it happen?"

"He's in serious condition," her father said. "But he'll make it. He was feeding the horses last night and fell over in the barn. Mom found him and called the paramedics right away. I've got to cancel my appointments and get on a plane to San Jose."

Her father picked up the phone again and started making reservations. "I want to go with you," Janet said to him. "I want to see Grandpa."

Suddenly, it seemed more important to her than anything else—school, training Storm. Anything.

"Janet, I think you should stay here with me," her mother said. "Your father will be back in a few days."

"But it's almost Christmas," Janet said. "I don't want Grandma to be alone."

The thought of her grandfather in a hospital bed brought tears to her eyes. The thought of her grandmother all alone in the house on Christmas Day made her cry outright. "There's only one more day of school left before Christmas vacation. I want to go. Please?"

In the end, her parents agreed. Her mother had to stay in Pasadena for a few days to finish up a deadline. But on Christmas Eve, Janet and her father would meet her at the airport. In the meantime, Janet would go to San Jose with her father.

"You may be alone in the house a lot," her father said. "I don't want you coming to the hospital every day and staying there all day."

"It's okay, Dad," Janet said. "I can feed the animals and take care of the ranch. That way, you and Grandma can take care of Grandpa and make sure he gets better. You won't need to worry about me."

Her father smiled and gave his daughter a big hug. "Thanks a lot, Scooter. That means a lot to me, how much you want to help out."

Janet had almost finished packing when she realized that there was just one problem with her plan: she had no way to get in touch with J.G. and Larissa to tell them she wouldn't be coming for a few days. Christmas was on Monday, and it was only Wednesday. At the earliest, she and her parents wouldn't be back until the following Tuesday. And the Gradys didn't have a phone.

She didn't want them to wonder what had happened to her, but how would she let them know? Finally, she came up with a solution. She found an old postcard she'd bought when she first moved to Pasadena, one she planned to send to Sarah, a friend up north. On the back, she wrote a note to Larissa and J.G.:

Hey guys! I have to leave town—it's an emergency. But I'll be back next week. Merry Christmas, and say hi to Storm for me. Whoops, I mean Lady!
Love, Janet

Janet wasn't sure how to address the postcard, since J.G. and Larissa didn't exactly live on a normal street, with numbers and everything. She settled on "Larissa and J.G. Grady, The Grady Ranch, Lower Arroyo Seco, Pasadena, CA" and hoped that the mail carrier would figure out how to deliver it.

Janet thought about her grandfather the whole way up to San Jose, but when she was actually standing in his room, she wasn't prepared for what she saw. Grandpa's face was pale, and it looked as if there were tubes and plugs attached to him everywhere.

"Janet," her grandfather said hoarsely when he saw her at the foot of his bed. "How's that mare of yours? Still giving you trouble in reverse?"

"Not anymore," she said, her eyes filling with tears to see her grandfather like this. "How're you doing, Grandpa?"

"Been better, kiddo. But I plan to get back on a horse again, you can be sure of that. They may have kicked me, but I won't stay down."

Her grandmother came into the room. "Janet!" she said. "I didn't know you were coming."

"I wanted to surprise you, Grandma," Janet said, giving her a big hug. "Merry Christmas."

"Merry Christmas," her grandmother said, returning Janet's hug. "I'm so glad to see you."

Janet stayed until visiting hours were over. Then she and her father and grandmother drove back to the ranch. They were quiet on the drive. Janet could tell that her grandmother was tired and that her father was preoccupied. Even if they had wanted to talk, she didn't know what she'd have to say. They were all thinking the same thing anyway: how hard it was to see her grandfather like that and how much they hoped he was okay.

Back at the ranch, they ate an early dinner of cold chicken. Janet's grandmother went to bed very soon afterward, leaving Janet and her dad to watch sitcoms on TV. It felt strange to be sitting in her grandparents' living room without her grandfather in his favorite chair. Janet tried not to think about it too much, though. She was going to take care of the ranch tomorrow, and that would keep her busy—too busy to think, she hoped.

"Oh, I forgot to tell you," her father said, interrupting Janet's thoughts. "Remember that conversation you had with Leonard a while back about ranchers in the arroyo? Remember how he said it might make for a good piece in the paper?"

"Sure I do," Janet said, thinking immediately of J.G. and Larissa. Would they get her note? She sure hoped so.

"Well, I guess his editor agreed," her father went on. "Turns out there's some pretty fascinating history about the place. He wrote up a little piece, and they ran it the other day. I have it here for you somewhere." After searching through his briefcase for a while, her father came up with the clipping. "Here you go."

Janet skimmed the headline. "'Pasadena's Arroyo Seco: Romance and Mystery in the Spirit of the Wild West,'" she read aloud. As she got further into the article, she was even more excited. "It says here that there really were ranchers down in the arroyo," she told her father. "They had cattle and sheep, and they even raised horses for the local farms in the San Gabriel Valley."

"Hmm," her father said, looking at the TV. "That's interesting."

Since Janet could tell that her father wasn't particularly interested, she read the article to herself. It said that originally there had been one ranch, given to a local farmer by the Mexican government in the early 1830s. After that, the rancher divided up the land among his four children. Then she got to something that made her heart beat faster.

One of the children had married a man whose last name was Grady.

"In the mid-1800s," the article continued, "John Grady gave up ranching and sold the land to his brother, who farmed the land into the late 1800s until the spectacular hundred-year flood of 1893 wiped out all the Grady holdings, leaving the family destitute. Legend has it that the waters rose so quickly that the Gradys were able to take only the shirts on their backs and nothing else."

Janet wanted to know more, much more, but for some reason, the article ended there. Leonard hadn't included what had happened to the Gradys or their ranch afterward. He didn't say anything about Larissa and J.G., or the fact that there was a ranch there now. Maybe he didn't know about it. Or maybe he didn't think it was important. But Janet did. She wanted to know how

J.G. and Larissa were related to the original Gradys. She figured they must be the great-grandchildren of the original ranchers. Why didn't the article mention them?

Janet shivered. It was as if the ranch didn't even exist anymore.

CHAPTER TWELVE

A hard rain pelted the window next to her bed. Somewhere off in the distance, there came the sound of neighing—a long, sharp whinnying noise that rose above the rain.

Someone had left the barn open! The horses were loose.

Janet felt the urge to get out of bed. She had to save them.

The horses were crying because they needed her. And Janet was the one in charge. She was the only one who could help. The neighing got louder and louder. They were in trouble. They needed her to come and help.

But she couldn't. Her legs felt like lead. She couldn't move. Something heavy was holding her down. When she tried to open her eyes, she couldn't. It was as if they were sealed shut.

VICKI KAMIDA

"Janet!" came her father's voice. "Janet, honey, wake up. Grandma and I are leaving for the hospital."

Janet awoke with a start. She looked out the window. The sun was shining, and the sky was clear. There was no rain. No horses.

"It was a dream," she told herself. "Just a dream."

Even so, the desperate feeling stayed with her. Those animals needing to be rescued, crying out in the dark night.

"You sure you'll be okay?" her grandmother asked. "You can always call the neighbors if you need anything."

"I'll be fine," Janet said. *If I can only get this darn dream out of my head,* she thought.

From the state of things around the ranch, it looked as if her grandmother hadn't had the strength to take care of things the way her grandfather would have. Neither did Janet, really, but she knew what to do from following her grandfather around. First, she mucked out all the stalls—even the pigpens—and made sure that all the feed and water were fresh. Then she saddled up Damsel, who had weaned her filly by now, and rode her out to the edges of the property to check on the fences. There were still a few head of cattle grazing out on the back pastures. Janet made sure none of them were sick or injured and left them to graze there.

Every once in a while, the dream came back to her. *It's probably nothing more than worrying about Sugar,* Janet thought. She still hadn't accepted that the gelding

142

probably wouldn't be coming back. The dream must have been telling her that she still felt guilty about what she'd done.

Back at the ranch house, she cleaned up the kitchen and living room. She was running the vacuum when the phone rang. It was her mother, checking in.

"I'm coming up tonight," she said. "We finished the project early."

"Hooray!" Janet was glad. She liked to be helpful, but she didn't really enjoy the idea of being alone all day. "I can't wait."

With her grandfather sick and Janet taking care of the ranch, Christmas passed in a blur. By the time they were about to go back to Pasadena, her grandfather was doing much better and would be ready to leave the hospital in a few days. Her grandmother's spirits were lighter, too, and as she kissed Janet good-bye, she told her how utterly grateful she was to Janet for all her hard work.

"I guess Grandpa was right," she said, rumpling Janet's hair as she got into the car. "He said you've got ranching in your blood. I think he knows what he's talking about."

Janet smiled. She'd had a great time taking care of things around the property. It almost felt as if she was in charge, and she took the job seriously. The stables were in fine shape, there was plenty of hay in the barn, and on Damsel she'd actually managed to move the cattle to the next pasture over when the grass had gotten lean.

"Grandpa would be proud of you," her grandmother said. "I am, too."

"Thanks, Grandma," Janet said. "You sure you'll be okay until Grandpa gets home?"

"Positive," she said. "Besides, Jim Clemson's coming over tomorrow to see to things. He's not nearly as handy as you are, but he'll do until I've got Cam back."

It had hardly felt like Christmas until Janet saw her grandmother smile. But once she did, she knew that everything would be okay.

"Janet!" J.G. cried. "Long time no see! Where'd you get to? Larissa and I were worried."

Janet had rushed over to the ranch as soon as she and her parents got home. Now she stood at the door to the barn, watching J.G. wrestle with a heavy barrel. The rain was coming down hard again, and there was more than one leak in the roof.

"Didn't you get my note?" Janet asked, helping J.G. with the barrel.

"What note?" J.G. asked, confused.

"I had to go to San Jose," Janet said. "My grandfather was sick. But I sent you a postcard so you wouldn't worry."

J.G. scratched his head. "We haven't gotten mail in a while," he said. "I think the post office lost track of us or something. I guess we should try to set them straight." He laughed. "Imagine how the bill collectors must feel. It's like we disappeared or something."

"I guess that's pretty convenient," Janet agreed. "I know my dad wouldn't mind not getting a bill or two." Then she remembered what J.G. had said about how he and Larissa were worried. It felt good to know they cared. "I missed you guys," she said.

"We missed you, too."

There was a long pause. Janet met J.G.'s gaze and tried not to wonder how much he had missed her. "How's Storm?" she asked, looking for an excuse to change the subject. After all, she didn't know how long she could stare into J.G.'s eyes without blushing.

"Tell you the truth, Janet, this rain has her spooked. We haven't been able to saddle or ride her since it started. I was hoping maybe you could do something with her."

J.G. led the way to Storm's stall. As soon as she took one look at the mare, Janet knew exactly what J.G. was talking about. Storm was restless in her stall, not with her usual prancing back and forth, but with a kind of anxious pacing. Her eyes were black and wild, and her chest heaved.

"Hey, hey," Janet said, trying to soothe the animal. "It's just me. Shush—"

She reached out to pet Storm's forehead, but the mare backed away from her touch with a high-pitched whinnying sound.

Janet was shocked. "I've never seen her like this."

"It's the rain," J.G. said, shaking his head sadly. "She's been like this ever since it started. The more it rains, the worse she is. You should see her when it pours. We have to tie her down and bandage her legs to keep her from hurting herself."

Janet tried to hide her concern and disappointment. She was worried about Storm, but she also felt bad that she wouldn't be able to saddle her up and get her back into shape. With only six weeks left before the season opener and all this rain, she wouldn't have time.

J.G. must have noticed her frustration. "Don't worry," he said. "The rain's got to stop sometime. It can't go on forever, right? Unless this is some kind of hundred-year flood or something."

J.G. was right, of course. This was California. When it rained, it felt as if it would never stop. But it did, eventually, and then the sun came out and everything dried up in about five minutes. But what J.G. said about the flood reminded her of Leonard's article.

"Hey," she said. "I read something about your ranch in the paper."

"You did?" J.G. sounded surprised. "What did it say?"

"That your family ranched this land from the early 1800s, and that the great flood forced you out," Janet said.

"Is that what it said?" J.G. smiled. "I guess whoever wrote that didn't get their facts exactly straight. Remember how I told you that the flood took my father's life and my mother's?"

Janet nodded.

146

"Well, my uncle and Larissa and I came back and took up ranching again. This land had been in our blood for a century. We weren't about to give it up."

So that was the explanation for why the article didn't mention the fact that the Gradys had come back. "I knew that," she said. "Maybe I can tell Leonard to come interview you so that he can add to the article."

"Who's Leonard?" J.G. asked.

"Just someone who works with my dad," Janet explained. "The guy who didn't get his facts straight."

J.G. laughed. "Well, I'd be happy for him to settle things right, but I don't really have time to talk to any old newspaper man. Why don't you straighten him out, Janet? Just pretend he's this ornery horse here."

"And wait for a clear day with no rain, right?" Janet countered.

"You got it," J.G. said.

J.G. had been right about Storm and the rain. Even on the days when it was just drizzling, there was no way Janet could get the mare to ride properly. She'd saddle her up and lead her into the corral, but as soon as she mounted her, the mare turned sour. She bucked and tried to throw her off even when Janet asked her to perform the simplest moves.

And the longer the rain went on, the worse things got. First, Storm went off her feed. Next, she tore up her stall so badly that J.G. had to put her in leg bandages and tie her down again. It was the strangest thing Janet had ever seen. She'd known horses to get spooked by the weather and by strangers or thunderstorms. But never by a spell of rain.

Even so, she knew not to fight it. Eventually, the weather was sure to clear. It had to. And eventually, she'd get back on Storm and put her into shape for the event. She just wished the weeks weren't passing by so fast. Soon it would be the end of January. That gave her only another month to train Storm. She was running out of time.

But still the rain didn't let up. She'd never known it to rain so hard or for so long. Everyone said it was unusual, even for Southern California, where January and February were the wettest months. There would be a few dry days, and Janet would get her hopes up about training Storm. Then the skies would darken, the clouds would come in, and the rain would start again. Sometimes they went a whole week without seeing a clear sky. At the stables, all the other riders got restless, too. Even on the clear days, the practice rings were muddy from the weather, and the horses couldn't get decent footing.

By now, the creek was dangerously high. It was becoming more and more difficult to cross. One night, Janet came home to the news that there had been a flood watch issued for the areas surrounding the arroyo and that emergency evacuations were planned.

"What do you mean, flood watch?" Janet asked her father, whose eyes were peeled to the small television set in the kitchen.

"Apparently anyone on high ground is safe," her father said. "But those people living in the lower arroyo are being told to pack up. The reservoirs are full, and the creek is probably going to overflow its banks. Maybe even tonight."

"You're kidding."

Janet heard the news as if it came from far away. It had been another impossible afternoon with Storm. The mare wouldn't even take a saddle and Janet was beginning to worry that she'd never get back on her. By the time she got home, she was wet and frustrated and barely able to pay attention to the TV set. But she made herself watch. There was a news crew down at the stables, which was on fairly low-lying ground. In the crowd, she spotted Connie rushing about in her yellow slicker, leading horses from their stalls.

"I've got to get down there," she said. "I've got to help."

"You're not going anywhere," Bob Marshall said. "This is serious, Janet. Look at that weather. They're talking about having to let some overflow out of the reservoirs so that the people on the higher ground aren't in danger, too. If that happens, the whole arroyo and everyone near it is in danger."

The rain flew sideways across the screen as the TV

crew filmed Connie and the others. She didn't see Hallie or Aloe or Becky, so she supposed that Connie had sent everyone but the adults home.

"Dad, please," she said. "I can't just sit here and watch."

"That's exactly what you're going to do," her father said, his voice firm. "No one is to leave this house tonight."

Janet kept her eyes focused on the TV screen. As she watched, another horrible thought came to her. The stables were on low-lying ground, but the ranch was down in the arroyo itself. There was no way J.G. and Larissa would be safe. But there was also no way that her parents were going to let her leave.

That night, Janet went to bed restless and upset. The rain wasn't letting up, and she was worried about J.G. and Larissa. She hoped they'd know to lead the animals to higher ground, but what if they didn't?

When she finally fell asleep, she had the worst nightmare of her life, much worse than the dream she'd had in San Jose. She dreamt that Storm was trapped in the arroyo and that Larissa was trying to save her but couldn't. The girl and horse were trapped on the sheer face of the canyon wall and could not get down. While Janet watched Larissa struggle, she heard another strange neighing, one that came from far off. It wasn't Storm, but another horse. A horse that was trapped and needed to be rescued.

She woke up sweating. Her heart was beating fast, as

fast as the rain outside. She knew what she had to do. Somehow, she had to get down to the ranch. J.G. and Larissa needed her help. She was sure of it.

When she got to the creek, Janet saw that the threat of flooding was serious. The water was rising in its banks, and, even in the dark, she could see how dangerous the muddy, fast-moving current would be. She shone her flashlight beyond the creek to the other side. There just had to be a way across.

She hiked down the creek, searching for a place where it was narrower and she might be able to get across. The idea was more than risky. It was dangerous and insane. But she had no choice.

Finally, she found a spot where she'd only have to cross ten feet or so of creek. She took one step into the creek and felt the waters pushing her along. It would take all her strength not to get swept away. She took another step, found her footing, and sank down to her waist.

Easy, Marshall, she told herself. *So long as you can feel the bottom, you're safe.*

Maybe. The current came close to sweeping her off her feet. But she pushed herself hard against it and kept trudging along. Soon she was halfway across. The creek was still only at her waist, a good sign. So long as she was above water, she could keep her balance and get to the other side.

She was three feet from the other bank. Then two.

Finally, she could actually reach out and grab a handful of dirt and rocks on the other side. The slope was slippery and it was hard to get a grip, but at last Janet had enough leverage to pull herself onto dry land.

By now, she was several miles downstream from the ranch. It took her a lot longer to reach the meadow and the path that led to the ranch. As she came upstream, she noticed a scary sight. To her right, the banks of the creek should have been at least a hundred yards off. Instead, she could hear the water rushing by, right next to the path. The closer she got to the ranch, the closer the banks were running. She knew that one part of the creek curved toward the ranch and that it forked off up toward the canyon. Now it looked as though the two branches were trying to merge and that the rains were making the two forks flood the land in between. Exactly where the ranch was.

By the time she got to the path that led to the ranch, the ground under her feet was covered in a foot of water. Farther down the path, the flooding got worse. Soon there was two feet of water, and soon after that she was wading through water that came to her knees. All around her, the water was rising. Debris came floating toward her on the current: buckets, farm tools, a hat of J.G.'s she recognized.

Janet tried not to panic, but the truth was, she'd never seen a flood firsthand. Until that night, she didn't know how fast the waters could rise, as if they were coming from beneath the ground itself. What would she do if she didn't find Larissa or J.G.? Would she be able to get back, or would she be trapped here?

The corral was under three feet of water. The rails she had once used to train Storm floated by. The water rose above the porch of the ranch house.

She pushed through the current to the house and peered inside. Empty. Some clothes were strewn around and the table was barely cleared from dinner.

In the barn, the stalls were flooded, the feed and grain floating in a sea of muddy water. The animals were gone. Storm's stall was empty.

"J.G.!" she cried. "Larissa!"

There was no answer. The ranch was empty, and Janet was alone.

Maybe they knew about the flood and had time to escape, Janet thought. *Maybe they are safe.*

And maybe you should get out of here, she told herself. *Fast!*

The longer she stayed, the more she was in danger. Even as she stood, the waters were still rising and the rain was still coming down. Crossing the creek was going to be even more dangerous this time.

Get out of here, Marshall. There's nothing you can do.

And then she heard it—the woeful sound of neighing off in the distance. It was just like her dream. Only this time, it was real.

CHAPTER THIRTEEN

*I*t's *Storm,* Janet thought. *She needs my help.*

She rushed straight from the corral in the direction of the mare's calls. From what Janet could tell, it sounded as if she were up close to the canyon. She could even have gotten trapped there, looking for dry ground.

The closer she got to the canyon walls, the louder the neighing became. Janet went as fast as she could, panicked about saving Storm. But as she waded upstream and deeper inland, the waters rose, too, making it hard for her to hurry.

When she got to the canyon, she saw that the fork of the creek that ran between the ranch and the canyon was about to overflow. On the near side of the fork, where Janet stood, the ranch and its headlands were rapidly taking in the creek's overflow. On the other side, the creek rushed furiously past the canyon's walls. Ten feet up, clinging to a small outcropping, Janet spotted the mare.

"Storm!" she cried.

"Janet!" a voice called out.

It was Larissa.

The girl stood next to Storm, clinging fiercely to the outcropping.

Janet froze. The image was just like the one in her dream. It was so strange to see it all over again: the rain, the flood, Storm trapped on the canyon walls, Larissa trying to save her.

Larissa had one hand on Storm's bridle. With the other, she was trying to keep her balance while she coaxed the animal down off the canyon wall. Obviously, Storm had gotten trapped there, looking for higher ground. Now she couldn't get down. Between the rain and the slick rocks and the rising creek below, it was an impossible task.

"Help!" Larissa said. "I can't get her down."

There was no time to waste. She had to get Larissa and Storm out of there before they were trapped. Without a second's hesitation, Janet plunged into the creek. The waters came up to her chest. She pounded through it, avoiding the branches, rock, and other debris the current had dragged down from the mountains. More than once, the water swept over her. But each time, she came up fighting for air, more determined than ever to make it to the other side.

Finally, she could feel the bank rise beneath her feet. She stumbled out of the creek, clawing at the dirt and rocks on the other side.

"Hurry!" Larissa urged. "I don't think I can last much longer."

"I'm coming!" Janet cried. "Hold on!"

She began to climb the canyon wall, grasping for handholds and footholds as she went. It was slow going. The rocks were slippery, and the hard-driving rain made it difficult to see her way. Finally, Janet was within a foot or two of Larissa. "Give me your hand," she said in relief.

Larissa hesitated. Janet could see the fear in her face. "Give me your hand," she insisted. "I'll help you down, and you can pull Storm behind you."

Horses could be stubborn, but in this case Janet knew that she and Larissa had gravity on their side. If they could get Storm off the outcropping, she'd have no choice but to stumble down the canyon wall. It was either that or fall, and Janet knew the mare would much rather stumble along than drop straight down into the creek.

Larissa held out her left hand to Janet, keeping a tight hold on Storm's bridle with her right. Because Larissa couldn't see below her, Janet guided her to the nearest footholds. As Larissa stepped forward, Janet backed up. At first, Storm bristled and held firm, but Larissa yanked hard on her bridle while Janet kept her hand gripped tightly around the girl's. Finally, Storm saw that she had no choice but to follow. Janet looked up to see the mare making her way gingerly down the steep face of the canyon wall. Rocks and gravel shot out from her hooves, but she kept her footing.

"She's coming," Larissa cried in relief. "We've got her."

"Not quite," Janet said, once they were at the base of the canyon wall. "We still have to get across that."

Janet could tell from just one look that in the time she'd spent rescuing Larissa and Storm, the creek had risen even more. It had crested its bank. Janet and Larissa found themselves standing right at the creek's edge.

"We can do it," Janet insisted. "Storm can swim, can't she?"

Larissa looked at the muddy, fast-rushing waters. Her gaze was more than skeptical—she was afraid. "I don't know," she said. "The rain's spooked her already. I have no idea if she'll go in."

"We've got no choice," Janet insisted. "Either she's going in or we'll be trapped back here. That creek's not going down. The only trail out of here is on the other side, back through the ranch."

Larissa swallowed and nodded her head. Janet was surprised to see the girl so afraid. Being stuck on the canyon wall with the mare must have spooked her. She had a far-off look in her eye and didn't seem able to help her come up with an escape plan. Janet could see it was up to her to make sure they got out of this alive.

She went to the mare and tried to calm her. Storm's

black eyes were clouded with fear. Her nostrils flared and she reared as soon as Janet reached out to touch her.

"It's okay, girl," she said. "We're going to get out of here. I promise. You just have to calm down a bit."

Storm whinnied and bucked harder, trying to back away. But Janet squared her legs, grabbed on to the mare's bridle, and put all her weight against Storm's. After a few hard tugs, Storm realized she had no choice. Janet was going to get her into the creek if it killed her.

Once she got the mare closer to the creek, Janet held on to Storm's bridle with one hand and went to give Larissa a leg up with the other. "Come on," she said. "You've got to mount her."

Larissa was still acting as if she were in a trance. "What?" she asked. "Ride across that?"

"How else are you getting over?" Janet asked. "You can't fly."

She practically shoved Larissa up on to Storm's wet back, grabbing on to her at the last minute to make sure she didn't slide off the other side. After Larissa was safely aboard, Janet also mounted Storm, squeezing into a spot in front of the older girl.

"Ready?" she said, turning to make sure Larissa was okay.

Larissa nodded grimly.

"Here goes nothing," Janet said.

Without a second thought, Janet dug her heels into Storm's belly.

The animal reared on its hind legs, still trying to back away from the creek.

"Whoa!" Janet said. "Hold on!"

She dug her heels in again, this time even harder. This time, Storm took the cue and plunged into the creek.

As soon as she entered the cold, muddy waters, Storm began to flail. Janet kept her hands tight on the reins, but she knew there was no way to control the mare. At this point, they were at the mercy of her footing and the creek's current.

Storm lost her balance, treading sideways, then pitching forward. The creek took them rapidly downstream, with Storm riding the creek nose forward. Janet dug in her heels, hoping to urge the mare to grab some footing, turn sideways again, and swim against the current. Behind her, Larissa was screaming in her ear. "Do something!" she shouted. "We're going to drown!"

"Not if I can help it," Janet said through gritted teeth. "Come on, Storm. Fight back! Swim! I know you can do it."

At last, Janet felt the animal resist the current. She wheeled around in the water, setting herself sideways against the stream. Beneath her legs, Janet could feel Storm's muscles straining to hold her ground and keep her position. Her neck jutted forward, and her body heaved from the effort.

"Good girl," she said. "Come on. Keep it up!"

Janet was just about to dare to hope that they might actually make it to the other side when, in the distance, she heard another mournful cry. The whinnying came from behind them, and it sounded as if another horse was trapped up in the canyon.

"What on earth is that?" Janet asked. "Is one of J.G.'s horses trapped back there?"

"I don't know," Larissa said. "Don't look back. Just get us across!"

But Janet had to look. If there was another animal trapped in the arroyo, she couldn't just let it drown. Her dream came back to her, yet again. She remembered another animal calling out to her...

She handed Larissa the reins. "Be careful," she urged. "Keep them tight."

Janet felt Storm grapple with the rocks on the creek bed, deep beneath her feet. She took her eyes off the mare for a moment, turned around, and saw a horrifying sight. A horse was barreling downstream, headed right toward them.

It was Sugar! The gelding was barely alive, struggling for his life.

"Larissa, quick!" Janet cried. "That's Sugar, the missing horse. We've got to save him!"

"You've got to be kidding!" Larissa said. "We'll be lucky if we can get across on Lady."

"You stay on her!" Janet shouted. "As soon as Sugar swims by, I'll make a jump for his back."

"No," Larissa said. Her expression was determined. "It's too risky. There's no way we can save them both. Please don't try this, please—"

But Janet wasn't listening. Instead, she kept her eyes peeled on Sugar. The gelding flailed in the rapid water, shocked and afraid. Unlike Storm, who now seemed to have figured out how to fight against the current, Sugar was barely able to let himself be carried along. Even worse, he had no bridle or harness. Larissa was right. Trying to save Sugar was a suicide move, but Janet had no choice. Of all the horses in the world she couldn't stand to lose, Storm would be the first. But Sugar came in a not-very-distant second.

"You can handle it," she told Larissa. "Hold on to her reins and keep steering her toward the bank. Okay. Ready? Hold on! I'm going for it."

There would only be one shot, one moment when Sugar was right next to them. After that, it would be too late. Janet held her breath, timed the move, and waited. Closer. Closer. The gelding tossed about in the water, just a few feet behind. A second more, and he'd be abreast of them…

With a yell, Janet leapt from Storm's back, reached out, and grabbed for Sugar. The gelding stared at her with a wild look—eyes rolled back, the whites showing. Janet's hand reached for his neck, her fingers clawing at his mane. The horse shuddered beneath her and dragged her along, but Janet had him. She was on board!

"You did it!" she heard Larissa cry. "Way to go!"

With her last remaining ounce of effort, Janet swung her right leg up and over the gelding's back. She dug her heels into the gelding's side, hoping to steer him toward the bank. Sugar turned around and gave Janet another helpless look.

"You can do it," she urged him. "I know you can."

Beneath her legs, Janet could almost feel Sugar's ribs. Wherever he'd been, he hadn't eaten much. The horse was weak from hunger and unable to fight hard, in spite of Janet's efforts with her legs at his sides and her hands on his mane. She looked behind her and saw that Larissa had managed to steer Storm nearly to the bank of the creek.

"Come on, Sugar," Janet said. "Don't let them show us up. One last fight, I promise, and then it's pastureland for you. I'll tell Connie to give you early retirement. No more lessons, no more training. Come on."

Janet could hear the desperation in her voice. If she couldn't get the horse under control, he'd drag them both down the creek. She dug her heels into his sides again, favoring her right leg, hoping Sugar would find some way to steer himself to the left. Then she pulled on his left mane with all her might. Sugar whinnied and bucked, but he took the cue. She could feel him fighting beneath her legs to regain control. Finally, she could tell that his muscles were going to work, that he was going to fight against the creek. Instead of bouncing along on the current, he dug his hooves in and found his footing.

"That's it!" Janet cried. "You've got it."

And he did. Slowly, Sugar found a way to fight back against the creek. At last, he was able to turn sideways and move slowly to the other bank. It was slow going, but Janet kept her heels dug in, her body low, and her hands tight on his mane. All along, she spoke encouraging words into his ear.

"You can make it," she said. "I know you can. Come on, Sugar, just a few more feet. Come on, you can do it."

Finally, the gelding found the creek bank beneath his feet and stumbled up to safety. As soon as they were on solid ground, Janet slipped from Sugar's back and collapsed. Larissa and Storm had already come ashore and were waiting for them.

"We did it!" she said to Larissa. "We saved them!"

"You did," Larissa said. "It was you, Janet. I couldn't save Lady by myself. We were trapped on that ledge. We both would have drowned if you hadn't come along and rescued us."

With a shiver, Janet realized that Larissa was right. "I had a dream that you and Lady were trapped in the arroyo," she said. "When I woke up, I knew that I had to come down to see if you were all right. The ranch is flooded, Larissa." Janet took a deep breath. "J.G.'s gone."

"I know," Larissa said. "As soon as the water started rising, we realized we had to save the animals. J.G. went out to the far pasture to take the cows up to higher ground. I went to the barn to get the animals. When I got there, I saw that Lady was missing. I tracked her up into the canyon. I was trying to get her down, but she kept wanting to climb instead of face the creek." As she told her story, Larissa's eyes filled with tears. "I thought we were doomed, Janet. I thought everything down here was lost. But you saved us. You really did."

"I had no choice," Janet said, and she meant it. Storm was the most incredible horse she'd ever known, and Larissa and J.G. had become like family. "There's no way I'd ever let anything happen to Storm or to you."

Tears fell from Larissa's eyes. When Janet glanced up at the mare, she saw the strangest sight. Storm was crying, too.

"Well, what have we here?" a voice called out.

Janet looked up and saw a figure on the path. "J.G.!" she said, recognizing the boy. "You're safe!"

Larissa ran toward her brother, who had appeared on the path that came down from the outer pastures. "Janet!" he cried. "Larissa!"

J.G. rushed forward and grabbed them both into his arms in a big hug. "You're alive! I didn't think I'd find anyone when I got back."

"Janet saved me," Larissa said. "Lady and I were trapped up on that canyon wall. But she brought us down and got us across the creek."

Janet saw J.G.'s eyes fill with pride and gratitude. For a moment, he looked so serious, it seemed as if he might even do something crazy like bend down and kiss her. Janet was relieved when that moment ended and J.G.'s sparkling smile returned.

"So who's that animal there?" he asked, pointing at Sugar.

"That's the missing horse from the stables," Janet said. "Can you believe it?"

"Not a chance," J.G. said. "Where was he?"

"Good question." Janet still hadn't been able to figure out how and why Sugar had gotten into the creek, but she had a guess. "Chances are he crossed the creek and got stuck in the canyon lands on the other side," she said. "I guess when the waters rose, he was flushed out."

"Literally," J.G. said with a laugh.

Janet laughed, then grew serious again. It felt great to know that everyone was safe, including Sugar, but she knew they couldn't stay there for long. The creek was still rising, and the waters on the banks came up to Janet's knees.

"We've got to get Storm and Sugar out of here," she said. "We need to head back through the ranch and cross the other fork of the creek before we're trapped."

Janet reached for Storm's bridle, but the mare backed away. Downstream, the path led back to the ranch and safety. Upstream, the trail went deeper into the arroyo, the far pasture, and the canyon lands beyond it. Storm didn't seem to want to head back to the ranch. Instead, she turned to go off in the opposite direction, where J.G. had come from.

"Come on, Storm," she said. "Don't be so stubborn."

But the mare continued to back out of the clearing, headed in the wrong direction. Larissa took a few steps after her, then stopped.

"We can't let her go!" Janet said, pushing past J.G. and Larissa.

J.G. grabbed on to Janet's arm. "Janet, no. She wants to go home," he said.

"But the ranch is her home," Janet said, confused.

"Not really," J.G. said, looking after the horse. "The arroyo is her home. The pastures and the canyons. I think she knows that."

"She'll drown up there," Janet said. "She'll get trapped in the floodwaters."

"Actually, there's dry ground up there," J.G. said. "The flooding's worst right down here, between these two forks. Maybe Storm knows that. Maybe she doesn't want to stay trapped down here with all this water."

"I don't see how that's possible," Janet said. "The safest place for her is out of the arroyo. We can find a stall for her at the stables until you get the ranch cleaned up again."

"I don't know as that would work," J.G. said.

Janet watched as J.G. and Larissa let the mare back out of the clearing. She couldn't believe they were going to lose her. "No!" she said, chasing after the mare.

"Janet!" J.G. cried. "She wants to leave. Let her go!"

But she couldn't. Storm was her life. She'd never ridden a horse like her. She'd never even known a horse like her. It wasn't just the thought of the competition either. It was the way Storm made her feel, from the very first moment that she'd ridden her. The horse was magic, and she couldn't let her go. She just couldn't.

"Storm!" she cried. "Come back!"

The mare stood in the clearing for a last moment. Then she turned on her heels, gave a high, whinnying cry, and bolted. By the time Janet got to the spot on the path where Storm had just been, the horse was gone.

CHAPTER FOURTEEN

torm!" Janet cried, taking a last look. The mare was just a blur of white on the path now. She could just see Storm's powerful form canter up the path, into the pasture and beyond. And she knew, somehow, that J.G. and Larissa were right. The mare was going home, back to the wilds where she belonged.

Janet turned around, ready to tell the Gradys that she understood what they had meant. But the clearing was empty now, except for Sugar. J.G. and Larissa had vanished, too.

What on earth, Janet thought. *Where'd they go? What happened to them?*

Janet's heart started pounding. One minute, she'd been there with Storm and J.G. and Larissa. The next, it was just her and Sugar. What was going on? She looked around but saw only the cold, dark night. Except for the rain, there was nothing.

"Larissa?" she cried. "J.G.? Where are you? Come on, you guys, this isn't funny!"

Janet shivered, waiting for them to answer. She glanced up at the canyon, then down along the path. Nothing. No shadows moving, no sound of anyone or anything except the creek and the rain. She came back to the clearing, looking behind the trunks of sycamores to see if maybe they were hiding. Of course, now wasn't exactly a good time to play some stupid game with her. But as far as Janet could tell, there was no other explanation for what was going on.

But they weren't hiding. They simply weren't there.

"What happened, Sugar?" Janet asked. Right now, the horse was the only thing she was sure of. "Where'd they go?"

The horse tossed his head and looked at Janet with his soft brown eyes. He didn't have an answer either.

"So they vanished, just like that," she said. "Into thin air?"

Yeah, right, Marshall, she said to herself. *Like ghosts, huh? Try explaining that one to Hallie or your parents.*

"J.G.!" Janet cried. "Larissa! We can't hang around here all day, you know. Come on!"

It was totally unlike J.G. or Larissa to pull a stunt like this. Even so, she didn't have time to stand around and wonder what had gotten into them. Around her, the waters were rising, getting deeper.

They must have headed back to the ranch, she thought.

Or had they?

Why didn't they say they were leaving? she wondered. *Why did they disappear so suddenly?*

There were a million questions running through her head, but right now she couldn't stand around thinking about them. She was in danger, and so was Sugar. The only choice was to head back to the ranch and look for J.G. and Larissa. After that, she'd have to lead Sugar across the other fork in the creek and back to safety. She didn't want to think about what she'd do if she still hadn't found the Gradys by then.

"Come on, boy," Janet said, holding Sugar under the nose. "Let's get you home."

Janet trudged through the rising waters with Sugar by her side. After swimming across the creek, wading through the muddy floodwaters was nothing. Beside her, Sugar was tense and nervous. It didn't help that he'd been stranded somewhere in the arroyo since before Christmas, nearly a month ago. The horse was painfully thin and obviously hungry.

"You'll be safe and sound and fed in no time," Janet said, trying to reassure him. "I'll bet you'll never be so happy to be back home in your stall." *Maybe this little adventure will even cure Sugar of his wandering ways,* Janet thought with a rueful smile. *He probably won't take to roaming too far from home, not after this.*

She didn't know what she'd find when she reached

the Grady ranch. Part of her must have been hoping that J.G. and Larissa would be waiting for her, as if nothing had happened. But when she led Sugar down past the barn and into the clearing in front of the house, the ranch was empty: no one stood on the porch, or in the corral, or by the barn. J.G. and Larissa were gone.

"J.G.?" she cried. "Larissa?"

She hunted through the barn and the house and came up with nothing. It was just her and Sugar, alone.

Janet had never felt so abandoned in her whole life. The Gradys had been her friends, like family to her. Now Storm was gone, and they'd gone off without even a good-bye. She started to cry. *Why?* she wondered. *What made them leave?*

She stood there for a long time. The rain came down and the waters rose. More debris floated by, including a shirt she recognized as J.G.'s. She waited and waited, confused and alone. Why had they left her? Why hadn't they said where they where going?

It didn't make any sense. Just before Storm disappeared on the trail, just before she'd gone after the mare and tried to stop her, J.G. had been so grateful. Larissa, too. She still remembered their hug. She'd rescued Storm and Larissa, and Sugar. Everything was going to be fine. So why had they just taken off like that?

When the waters were so high that Janet could no longer ignore them, she clucked at Sugar, who'd been searching the water for any food that floated by. "Time to leave," she told the gelding. "Time to go home."

✎✎

At the stables, the TV crews had packed up and left. Janet walked past the empty barns, unsure if Connie would still be there. But there was a light on in the office, and Janet spotted her boss as she led a last animal through the muddy waters toward a waiting horse trailer.

"Connie," Janet said. "Look who I found!"

"Janet!" Connie turned to see Janet leading an exhausted Sugar. "Sugar! Where was he?"

"You'll never believe this," Janet said, handing the horse over to Connie, who examined him in amazement.

Janet went on to tell Connie how she found Sugar down in the arroyo, floating along in the creek. She left out the part about J.G. and Larissa and Storm. She still didn't have any idea how she'd explain all that, especially the part about how the Gradys had let Storm run off back into the arroyo and how they'd disappeared themselves. Besides, she was still too upset that they'd just left her there.

"But what made you look for him there?" Connie said. "He's been missing for weeks. Why did you even think he was still alive?"

Janet hesitated. How could she explain? "Call it intuition," she said, coming up with the best possible answer. "I always had a feeling that Sugar might have crossed the creek. I just never thought, until tonight, that maybe it was worth looking for him over there. But I guess it was." She felt bad lying about her real reason for going across the creek, but there was no way she could tell Connie—or anyone else for that matter—the truth.

"I guess so," Connie said. She handed Sugar over to another trainer, who led the animal away. "Make sure he gets some feed," Connie instructed the trainer. "Not a lot to start with. And put a blanket on him and water him first," she said. "This horse has been through a major trauma. He'll need a good dose of TLC."

When Connie was through giving the trainer instructions, she looked back at Janet, shaking her head in amazement. "I can't believe it," she said. "You actually saved that horse. You're a hero, Janet."

"Not exactly," Janet said. "It was just luck."

"Well, whatever it was," Connie said, "you can be sure you'll be rewarded for it. Everyone at San Pascual is going to know about what you did. And if they're like me, they'll be impressed. Very impressed."

Janet waited until Connie had finished making sure that the stables were completely cleared out. The creek was still rising, and there was no telling how long it would be before the horses could safely return to San Pascual. In the meantime, the Equestrian Center in Burbank had found places for them, stalls where they would be safe and dry—and on high ground.

When the last horse trailer pulled out, with Connie in the driver's seat, Janet took a final look around. The red barns were empty, the rings ghostly and silent in the rainy night. She'd never felt so alone in her whole life.

～✦～

When she awoke the next morning, the sun was streaming through her bedroom window and the sky was clear. The rain had ended. She might have thought the night before was a dream, except that her wet clothes still lay draped across the chair by her desk, and her hair was still damp in the back, where she'd slept on it.

Downstairs, she found a note from her parents. They'd gone shopping and would be back later that afternoon. Leonard was coming over for dinner that night, so Janet should make sure to be home by six, no matter what.

Over her bowl of cereal, the same feeling of being lost and alone came over her. J.G. and Larissa were gone. So was Storm. But she still didn't understand what had happened or why.

Since her parents wouldn't be home until later, she quickly dressed in some clean, dry clothes. Then she put on her sneakers and a jacket and headed down into the arroyo.

The waters had subsided, but the flood had done its damage. Everywhere, debris lay scattered along the creek bank: leaves, branches, old rusted cans, and other garbage flushed out of the mountains. At the meadow, the grass was flattened and wet. Her sneakers sank into several inches of mud. The path that led back to the ranch had nearly been wiped out by the flood. If she hadn't taken it so many times already, she might have lost her way.

Above her head, blue jays jumped through the branches of the sycamore trees. In spite of the sunny skies and the warmth on her face, Janet's mood still felt more like the rain and flooding of the night before. Why had J.G. and Larissa abandoned her like that? Well, she intended to find out.

As Janet took the turnoff for the ranch, her heart grew even heavier. For some reason, she didn't hear the usual hum this time. That warm glow she'd always noticed before was gone. Sounds weren't crisper or louder, and the good feeling that always came over her whenever she stepped onto the path was absent.

As she crept up the path, she sensed that things were different. Maybe it was all the damage the flood had done. Farm equipment lay scattered all around. There was J.G.'s shirt, the one she'd seen the night before, but it looked weather-beaten and faded. Closer to the clearing, she saw that the storm and the flood had taken their toll on the buildings, too. Planks of wood had fallen from the barn's outside walls. The corral stood silent and empty, rails and posts missing, leaving big gaps in what had been the neat circle where she had trained Storm. She walked up onto the porch and peered inside. On the floor of the ranch house, clothing, pots, and pans lay scattered about. The table was set for dinner, two plates across from each other, but the hearth was cold.

"J.G.!" Janet called out. "Larissa!"

She stepped off the porch and walked toward the barn. There, the stalls were empty. The flood had washed away the animals' hay and feed. And somehow, in just one night, all the tools she'd seen J.G. and Larissa use had rusted.

Janet tried not to notice all the differences, but it broke her heart to see the ranch in such a shambles. J.G. and Larissa would have a huge job putting it all back together again.

If they ever come back, Janet thought grimly.

Of course they're coming back, Marshall, she told herself. *There's got to be an explanation for all this. Just you wait.*

She searched the entire ranch, telling herself the whole time that they'd show up again, that they'd simply headed for higher ground. They'd come back. They had to. But when she stood on the porch of the ranch house an hour later, weary and despondent, she had to admit that she'd run out of hope.

Her hand reached out and found the dinner bell, the one she'd seen J.G. ring to call Storm down out of the canyon the first time she'd been there. Janet rang it now, hoping that maybe it would call J.G. and Larissa to her. But the bell's sound was hollow, and when she stopped ringing it, the corral and the ranch were still empty and she was still alone.

Janet hiked out of the arroyo just as the sun was setting. It was an amazing night—clear and crisp—and the light cast soft shadows on the sycamores and sagebrush. She breathed in the familiar arroyo smells, the creosote and sage, and listened to the blue jays and crows call to one another as they soared through the sky. But for once Janet didn't appreciate the magic of the arroyo. She had to find some answers to what had happened to J.G. and Larissa.

Of course, she had no idea how she was going to get those answers. Right now, it was all still so confusing. And upsetting, too.

Back at home, her parents were sitting in the living room with Leonard, drinking coffee. She said a quick hello and was about to head to her room to get cleaned up for dinner when she remembered Leonard's article.

"My dad gave me that article you wrote," she said to Leonard now. "I was wondering…what happened to the ranch after the flood of 1893? It seemed strange that you didn't say."

"That's because my editor cut it from the story," Leonard said with a laugh. "Isn't that always the way, Bob? He tells you to give him a thousand words, next thing you know it's down to two-fifty and the whole gist of the piece is gone."

Her father smiled. "It's been known to happen. But he'll always say he only asked for five hundred in the first place."

"Exactly," Leonard agreed. "Actually, since you ask, Janet, there was another part of the story."

"The ranch was farmed again, wasn't it?" Janet asked.

Leonard seemed surprised. "Yes, it was," he admitted. "How did you know?"

"Just a hunch," she said sadly, thinking about Larissa and J.G.

"Well, Janet, your hunch was right," Leonard said. "A brother and sister worked it. They came back and kept the farm going with their aunt and uncle after their parents died."

"A brother and sister?" Janet asked. This wasn't exactly the information she expected. "What were their names?"

"J.G. and Larissa," Leonard said. "Why do you ask?"

It couldn't be, Janet thought. That would have been a hundred years ago. Leonard had to be talking about some other J.G. and Larissa. Maybe *her* J.G. and Larissa were named after their grandparents or something. "When exactly was this?" she asked.

Leonard thought for a moment. "End of last century, I believe. J.G. and Larissa Grady came back to farm the ranch after that first flood. But three years later, they were flooded out again. That was just about a hundred years ago. Come to think of it, nearly to the day of that flood last night."

But that was impossible. She'd seen J.G. and Larissa in the flesh, just the day before.

Until they vanished, that is.

Part of her didn't want to hear any more. What Leonard was saying didn't make sense. There was no explanation for it, except...

Part of her just had to know. "What happened this

time?" she asked. "Did they go back again? There must have been someone left to farm the ranch."

"I'm afraid not," Leonard said. "Apparently their uncle came back and found the ranch abandoned, the animals gone."

"And J.G.?" she asked. "Larissa?"

Leonard shook his head. "Gone."

Janet's heart began to pound. When she looked at her parents, she saw that they were staring at her. They must have been wondering why she was reacting this way. But there was nothing she could do to hide her feelings.

"Even the incredible horse that belonged to Larissa," Leonard was saying. "The uncle thought that maybe they'd gone to rescue the horse and got trapped in the arroyo. By the flood, I mean. I guess he claimed to see the horse every once in a while after that."

"Her horse?" Janet asked. "What kind of horse was it?"

Instinctively, she knew the answer would be more than she could take, but she had to know.

"A white mare," Leonard said, his voice low and mysterious. "A horse that rode like the wind."

"That's some story," Janet's mother said. "It gives me the shivers just hearing about it."

Janet felt her limbs go numb now. A low, sinking feeling came over her. If Leonard was right, it could mean only one thing.

She felt as if she were going insane.

They'd all been ghosts. Storm. J.G. Larissa. From the very start, they'd never been real.

But how was that possible? How did that explain the fact that she'd known them, talked to them? How could she have ridden Storm and even trained her if she wasn't a real, live horse?

Her parents looked really worried now. "Janet, what's wrong?" her mother asked. "You look like you've just seen a ghost."

"Maybe I have," she whispered.

Even so, she refused to believe it. Leonard *had* to be wrong. He just had to be. She thought about all the time she'd spent at the ranch, all the conversations she'd had. She'd even touched J.G.! And she'd saved Larissa and Storm from drowning. There was no way they were ghosts! There had to be another explanation.

Right, Marshall, she thought to herself. Just like there's another explanation for the fact that J.G. and Larissa had disappeared, just like that.

Vanished into thin air.

EPILOGUE

anet took a deep breath as she wheeled Sugar around to face the judges. The big day had come. On either side of her, other riders were lined up on their mounts.

"Okay, boy," Janet whispered, petting Sugar to keep him calm. "Here goes nothing."

One by one, the judges gave the riders their commands. "Turn the horse. Walk at a fixed gait. Put him to the trot. Change leads. Now canter. Drop your irons. Counter canter. Hand gallop. Return to a trot...."

The commands seemed to go on and on. Janet tried to concentrate on Sugar and her cues, and to keep her attention focused on her form. But it was hard not to watch the other riders to see how they were doing. Compared to some of them, Janet knew that her form was better. But Janet could tell that Becky was putting on a fine show, too. MacDougal looked great—his ears were perky, his steps even, and his transitions smooth. By the time the commands ended and the riders were told to halt and face the judges again, Janet was exhausted. The whole event had lasted maybe ten minutes, but they must have done at least two dozen moves.

From the stands, Hallie gave Janet a big thumbs-up. Hallie wasn't competing in this first class—junior novice eq—but was waiting for the junior limit eq class instead. After this first round, all three girls would compete in the eq for twelve- to thirteen-year-olds, the class the stables was sponsoring. Whoever qualified in that round would go on to compete in the medal class.

The riders waited as the judges added up their points. One by one, the winners were called, from last place to first. As they got to fourth place, Janet's hopes began to sink. She couldn't possibly do better than that. She must not have pinned at all.

"And in third place, rider number 67, Janet Marshall."

Janet's mouth dropped open, and she dropped her reins. From the bleachers, she saw her parents jumping up and down. "Way to go, Janet!" they cried. "All right!"

It felt great to have placed. Janet could hardly believe her luck. After everything that had happened, she actually had her first ribbon!

From that moment on, Janet knew she was going to be okay.

After his ordeal in the arroyo, she'd learned to be

more patient with Sugar. The horse needed tender loving care, and Janet felt that now they had a special bond.

They'd both been trapped in time down in the arroyo.

At least that was one way to think of it.

Once the skies had cleared and the waters had receded, Janet had taken a few trips down to the ranch. But each time she went, the place was still empty and abandoned. She'd never seen J.G. or Larissa or Storm again.

At night, as she fell asleep, she went over and over what had happened, from her first dream to that first time she'd seen J.G. and Storm. She remembered how J.G. had said they didn't have a phone. Then there was the business of how they didn't get mail. And he hadn't known what she meant when she said she was "grounded" either.

As she added up the confusing pieces of what had happened, she began to think that maybe Hallie's mother was right. Maybe time *was* a circle. Maybe somehow she'd gone halfway around, found J.G., Larissa, and Storm, then come back to the starting point where her own life began. Or maybe she'd dreamt the whole thing.

Except that she knew she hadn't. Sugar had been missing—and she really had trained Storm. Her horsemanship proved it. Even on Sugar, with his clumsy feet and his tendency to land on a left lead after every jump,

Janet was a better rider. She sat higher in the saddle. And now she knew what it meant to move with the animal, rather than against it.

Storm had taught her all this.

She still didn't understand what it all meant, but she was beginning to understand that since that very first night, Storm had meant for Janet to find her. At first, she thought that maybe she'd wanted a horse so badly, she dreamt Storm to life. But then she realized that Storm had needed her as much as she needed Storm. Hadn't she saved Storm, after all?

Leonard said that Storm used to haunt the arroyo like a ghost. Maybe it was Janet's job to put her spirit to rest, for once and for all. Wasn't that what happened when Storm went running back into the canyon lands the night of the flood? Hadn't J.G. said it? Storm wanted to be free.

So maybe Janet had set her free. Maybe the night of the first flood, Storm and J.G. and Larissa had all been trapped. Maybe by saving Storm, Janet had somehow managed to save them all.

She'd never believed in ghosts before, but she knew the feeling she'd had every time she'd set foot onto the path that led to the ranch. She'd always remember it.

And she'd never be able to explain it either.

The sound of the announcer's voice came over the loudspeakers and interrupted Janet's reverie.

Hallie took a first in her class, and Hallie, Becky, and Janet came in first, second, and third in the eq for twelve- to thirteen-year-olds. That meant that all three girls advanced to the special medal class to be held the next day.

Until now, Janet had felt really good about the competition. Of course, there was no chance she'd come in first or second in the medal class, which would mean a trip to the finals at Madison Square Garden in New York City, but even so, she was proud of how well she'd done.

But as soon as she saw the course, she knew that she and Sugar were jinxed. There wasn't just one in-and-out in the course, there were two. For the first time since the opener started, Janet thought again of Storm. On Sugar, there was no way she could place with that many in-and-outs, but on Storm, there would have been no problem. She walked away from the course discouraged.

When Janet's name was called and she entered the show ring riding Sugar, her fears were confirmed. The horse took one look at all the jumps and froze.

"Come on," Janet urged him. "You can do it. Please don't do this to me now, Sugar. Please."

She dug her heels into the animal's sides, hoping the judges weren't paying too close attention. It wasn't good form to shove your heels into your horse's belly. A quiet "cluck" was usually all that was required to get the horse going.

"You did it on Saturday," Janet told the horse. "I know you can do it again."

But Sugar still didn't want to move.

"Rider 67, are you ready?" the judge asked over the

loudspeaker. "You can proceed at any time."

Janet wanted to tell the judge that *she* was ready, it was her horse that wasn't. *What's wrong with me?* Janet wondered. She'd never had any problem getting Sugar going before. It was just when she got to the jumps that the gelding gave her a hard time.

The seconds passed, and the audience in the stands started to get restless. Why hadn't Janet started?

"Rider 67, please begin, or leave the ring."

Janet felt the tears well up in her eyes. She knew it was awful to lose her cool like this, but suddenly it felt as if everything that had happened in the past few weeks was crashing down on her all at once: the flood, losing Storm, having J.G. and Larissa disappear. Until this moment, she hadn't let herself think about how she'd feel not riding Storm in the season opener, after all their training. But with Sugar standing stock-still beneath her legs, and with the course laid out before her like this, ready to be taken, and a horse that couldn't do it, she was this close to falling apart for once and for all.

"Rider 67."

The judge was getting impatient. Janet looked to the stands, where her parents and the judges sat. All eyes were on her.

"Rider 67!"

If only J.G. were here, she thought. *Or Larissa.* If only she were riding Storm, and not Sugar.

But she wasn't. She was riding Sugar. And, a voice

told her, if anyone could make the horse move, it was her.

No one's as stubborn as me, she thought. *Not even this ornery gelding.*

All the training she'd ever had—from her grandfather, from Connie, and especially from Storm—came to her now. If she could teach a ghost horse how to back up without dumping her, there was no reason why she couldn't get Sugar over these jumps. Storm had been incredible, sure, but hadn't Janet been the one to teach her the moves?

She gathered the reins in a firm hand and coaxed Sugar into a trot. If she closed her eyes and dreamed hard enough, she could almost imagine she was riding Storm, controlling her, keeping her in form with her cues. All she had to do was hold on to that feeling.

"All right, Janet!" her mother cried. "Way to go!"

They were over the first jump!

From then on, at each jump, Janet just thought of how it felt to be riding Storm. It didn't matter if Storm was a ghost or real. She would always have that feeling of riding her. And that feeling alone could carry her through the toughest course in the world.

Janet cleared the whole course, including the in-and-outs, without a single false step or clipping a single jump. When she was done, her parents rose to their feet. Even Hallie was jumping up and down. They all knew that she'd turned in an incredible performance, one that no one had thought Sugar could pull off. Janet looked over to the judges' table and saw the three women shaking their heads in disbelief. This was the horse who couldn't even get started on the course?

Janet led Sugar out of the ring and waited for the other riders to take the course. Finally, it was time for the winners to be announced. The fifth- and sixth-place ribbons went to riders from the Equestrian Center. Two more San Pascual exhibitors took fourth and third. Janet stood next to Hallie, waiting for second place to be called.

"Rider 68, Hallie McGill."

Hallie squealed with delight. "That means you took first," she said, giving Janet a big hug before going off to accept her award. "Way to go, Marshall!"

Janet couldn't believe her friend could possibly be right. But when the next and last award was called, it was her name the judges announced.

"In first place, Burbank Equestrian Center Classic, riding Sugar, out of San Pascual Stables, Janet Marshall, rider 67. Congratulations, Janet."

Janet's legs shook as she walked Sugar back into the ring and toward the judges' table. She'd actually come in first! She was going to Madison Square Garden!

A cheer erupted from her parents and Hallie as she took the award and walked Sugar from the ring. Janet heard them calling out her name and clapping for her. It was then she knew what Storm had really given her: the chance to win this medal, her very first.

❧❧

Later that afternoon, after the horses had all been trailered back to the stables and groomed and fed for the evening, Janet took a last stroll with Sugar. She had her medal pinned to her jacket and kept looking at it to make sure it was real. She remembered that first day, training with Connie, Hallie, and Becky, and how her sights had been set on competing with Yankee. She'd come a long way since then, and so had Sugar.

"You're a good boy, aren't you," Janet said, clucking to the horse.

No one ever thought Sugar could win in a medal class. And maybe he wouldn't have been able to, if it hadn't been for her.

And Storm.

For the first time in weeks, Janet felt a tug pulling at her: the ranch, the arroyo. There was no real reason to go down there again. All her trips back had only confirmed the worst. J.G. and Larissa were gone, the ranch was abandoned.

But somehow she knew she had to go back this one last time. If nothing else, she wanted to stand in the clearing and tell J.G. and Larissa—wherever they were—about what had happened and that she'd never forget them. Ever.

When she was sure no one was looking, Janet hopped on Sugar's bare back. At first, the horse seemed surprised. "I know, I know," Janet told him. "It has been a long day, but there's just one last ride I think we should take—together."

The last few times she'd been to the ranch, she hadn't noticed any special feeling come over her when she stepped onto the path that led to the ranch. She knew now that the feeling was part of the whole ghost world she'd somehow stepped into. Now that J.G., Larissa, and Storm had all been set free, they weren't ghosts anymore. And there wasn't any special hum or neat light or orange glow.

Janet knew that was because the ghosts were gone. The ranch was just a ruined spot. Maybe someday some other girl would discover it and wonder what had happened there.

This time, she didn't expect it to be any different. And it wasn't. When she and Sugar stood at the edge of the path, she didn't feel anything. The magical hum and that special energy were still gone.

As she walked down the path, Janet tried not to think of the dozens of times she'd been here, to find J.G. and Larissa and Storm waiting for her. She didn't know how it was that she'd traveled between her own time and the ghost time where Storm and the Gradys were still alive. She knew that there was no point in trying to make sense of it.

At the clearing, the ranch and the corral and the barn were still in shambles. Wood, feed, and all sorts of debris lay scattered about. Janet thought about coming back and cleaning up the spot, but what was the point? J.G. and Larissa would never be back to see it.

Janet was convinced that once she'd saved Storm,

something had happened to make J.G.'s and Larissa's spirits disappear, too. She remembered that night of the flood, how the moment Storm had vanished up the trail, J.G. and Larissa had disappeared, too. Maybe that was the reason J.G. insisted that Janet let Storm go. He knew that they couldn't be free unless Storm was, too. If Leonard was right, and J.G. and Larissa had been trapped in the arroyo trying to save Storm, it made sense that their spirits would vanish when Storm was saved. Janet was guessing, but wasn't it possible that their fate was connected to Storm's in some important way? If that was the case, then they weren't coming back either.

Or were they?

Wandering around the ranch, she couldn't believe they were gone forever. She picked up one of J.G.'s shirts and dusted it off. What if she carried it home? Would it suddenly vanish as soon as she left the arroyo?

Janet laughed. *Still looking for proof, Marshall?* she asked herself. *Don't bother.*

She was taking a last look inside the ranch house when she heard Sugar neighing outside. She ran into the corral to find the horse spooked. The gelding was stamping his feet and rearing, trying to unhitch himself from a fence post.

"Oh, no, you don't," Janet said, rushing to calm him down. "I thought you were through trying to escape."

She reached out to calm Sugar, whose brown eyes looked at her in fear.

"What's wrong, kiddo?" Janet asked. "Seeing ghosts again?"

"Maybe he is," a boy's voice said.

"Or maybe not," a girl's voice added.

"J.G.!" Janet cried. "Larissa!"

She turned. She fully expected to see J.G., with his familiar smile, and Larissa standing next to the barn. But the clearing was empty.

"J.G.? Larissa?"

She was sure she'd heard their voices. And Sugar was definitely spooked.

"Are you here, or not?" she asked. "J.G., Larissa. Please, please, answer me."

The skies were getting dark now. In the wind, Janet could hear the birds calling overhead. It was time to go home, time to go back. There was no one here. Janet shivered. She'd been imagining things, that was all.

But then, among the sounds of the wind and the birds, she heard another sound farther off—the sound of hoofbeats, and then a neighing, a familiar whinnying cry. Storm. Then laughter. J.G.'s laughter.

And after that, she heard the familiar voices speaking softly to her, as if they came from a far-off place. It was a place Janet would never reach, but one that would be there for her, she guessed, forever.

"You did it, Janet," they said. "You set us free."

THE END

I'd like to thank Connie, Aloe, and Breezy, and all my other friends at the San Pascual Stables, for all their patience, cooperation, and enthusiasm. This book is for you, and for everyone else out there who has discovered what it means to ride and own and love a horse.

—Vicki Kamida